ESCAPE THE FALL

Nuclear Survival: Southern Grit Book Two

HARLEY TATE

ESCAPE THE FALL

Nuclear Survival: Southern Grit Book Two

After unthinkable, would you know what to do?

With a four-legged companion and no food in the pantry, Grant Walton faces an uphill battle. His wife is still missing, downtown is a smoldering crater, and radiation is killing more people every day. Torn between searching for his wife and gearing up for what's sure to come, Grant is forced to put more than his morals to the test.

A nuclear attack wounds long after the explosion.

Leah Walton escaped a nuclear bomb that flattened her hospital and vaporized her friends. Now she's racing to find her husband miles away. When her borrowed car ends up in a twisted, smoking heap, she wakes up injured and alone. She'll have to rely on the kindness of strangers to survive and hope none of them kill her in the process.

Could you drop everything to save yourself?

While Grant and Leah struggle to stay alive, the United States falls deeper into chaos. Bombs destroyed cities, but mankind will rip the country apart. Can Grant find his wife in a city of six million people? Can Leah survive until he does?

The attack is only the beginning.

Escape The Fall is book two in *Nuclear Survival: Southern Grit*, a post-apocalyptic thriller series following ordinary people struggling to survive after a nuclear attack on the Unites States plunges the nation into chaos.

* * *

Subscribe to Harley's newsletter and receive *First Strike*, the prequel to the *Nuclear Survival* saga, absolutely free.

www.harleytate.com/subscribe

* * *

CHAPTER ONE

LEAH

State Road 372
   North of Atlanta, Georgia
   Thursday, 9:00 a.m.

Cold morning air frosted Leah's cheeks as she leaned her head out the window. The biting sting contracted her pupils and forced oxygen to her brain. If she hadn't lived the past six days in the center of it all, she would never have believed it.

First, a high-altitude nuclear detonation took out the electrical grid for most of the East Coast. It sent downtown Atlanta into chaos. Cars crashed all over the road. Hospital equipment at Georgia Memorial stopped working. Leah powered through a twenty-hour shift and barely made a dent in the suffering.

If only that were the worst of it. People could survive without electricity, but the nuclear detonation on the ground changed everything. Flattening downtown Atlanta and almost everyone Leah knew, the weapon didn't care about hospitals or patients or babies clinging to life.

Leah swallowed. The top twenty-five cites in the United States were clogged with the dead and dying. Smoking and smoldering ruins sat where hubs of activity used to be. The blasts must have killed millions, and exposure to radiation would kill millions more.

She pulled her head back inside the ancient Buick and wrinkled her nose. Even with the windows rolled down, the stale whiff of cigarettes made her twitch. Thanks to an old man who cared more about sitcom reruns than survival, Leah had a car. She was lucky.

Sun glinted off the hood of the old station wagon and she blinked back a sudden rush of tears. If she blocked out the sight of a string of abandoned cars, Leah could almost pretend the country wasn't falling apart. She pulled the visor down and flipped open the mirror. No signs of radiation poisoning yet. Her blonde hair still waved in the wind. Her pale cheeks turned pink from the cold. Her eyes were clear and focused.

A concrete and brick bookstore had saved her life, and a handful of locals guarding a Walmart had kept her going. Now it was time to find her family. In a few hours, she would coast into Hampton, Georgia, hug her husband and sister, and thank God for small favors. As she turned a corner, the first open stretch of road in forever beckoned and Leah took advantage.

The Buick wobbled as she eased the accelerator to

near highway speeds. Her hair whipped against the seat back, the tears finally leaked from her eyes, and Leah glanced at the passenger seat. An air rifle sat on top of a duffel stuffed with food and drinks. *I'd trade it all for someone to talk to.*

As she returned her attention to the road, her gaze caught on the radio dial. What were the chances?

Leah turned it on, hoping against hope. *Static.* She spun the dial, frowning as the little red bar reached the end of the stations. *Nothing.* It had been hopeless from the start, but she longed for a human-generated sound. Music. Talk radio. Even meaningless advertisements.

With the world turning digital, she hadn't bought a CD in years. Did anyone even own a record player? So many songs. So many voices. All gone.

Glancing back at the radio, the rectangular opening beneath it caught her eye. The car was way too old for cassettes. Leah pushed the play button and music filled the cabin. Not the dowdy old standards she expected, but a raucous, upbeat, dance-in-your-seat disco track.

Leah laughed out loud as Donna Summer's voice rose above the rhythm. The vocals and the melody and the never-ending optimism brought back so many memories. Her mom dancing in the kitchen while she cooked Sunday dinner. Her father picking her up and spinning her around like the kids on *American Bandstand*. She turned the volume up and sang along, cruising down the street and away from Atlanta.

Leah thought about her sister's little town nestled forty miles away from the horror of downtown. Five thousand people tucked between rolling hills and a flowing river. They might not have electricity, but they would still have books and pianos and guitars.

Music could still spread joy. Hope filled Leah's heart as she smiled for the first time in a long while. The last few days would fade from her memory and the horror right along with it. She would survive. America would rebuild. She just had to have faith.

As the chorus crescendoed, Leah cranked up the volume. The dashboard rattled, the seat shook with each bass beat, and Leah shouted out the words. The road rose in front of her and Leah eased the gas pedal to the floor, forcing the Buick into the red line on the RPM. She almost felt like she was flying.

As the car nosed over the hill's crest, a noxious smell hit Leah's nose. She snorted and eased up on the gas.

A plume of smoke rose from the engine. The car shuddered.

Oh, no. Leah squinted at the dash. The engine temperature hovered in the critical zone. The smell of burning fluid and rubber and something nasty filled the car. A rush of smoke wafted over the hood and windshield. *Why didn't I notice? Why did I push the car so hard?* Every second the smoke increased, obscuring her view of the sloping road ahead. She fumbled with the wipers, trying in vain to clear the smoke enough to see.

The road dipped to a steeper grade and Leah applied the brake. She'd been going so fast, it would take forever to stop the car. She leaned out the window, trying to see. Through the smoke a shape loomed ahead.

Leah's eyes went wide. Something massive sat in the road, way too close and gaining. A garbage truck? A dumpster? Leah whipped the steering wheel, grabbing it hand over hand and cranking with all her might as she stomped on the brake.

The car shimmied and the brakes squealed and she lost control, spinning in a circle as the tires hit something slick.

The billowing smoke turned it all into a blind nightmare. She didn't know if she would clear the blockage or if the car would slam into it head-on. Panic closed her throat and sent her heart into overdrive, beating like a hummingbird against glass.

The car tipped with two wheels off the ground, and Leah screamed. Throwing her arms over her head, she ducked for cover as the rear of the station wagon slammed into something solid and unforgiving.

The metal crumpled inward, the rear window shattered, and the back seat buckled under the force. Leah's seat flew forward from the impact, slamming her shoulder into the dashboard before she bounced back against the cushion. Her head hit the door handle and she screamed again as her whole body flew like a marionette on strings.

Everything was spinning. The car, her vision, the world all around. This was it. She would survive a nuclear attack to die in a car crash while an 8-track cheered her on. Leah opened her eyes as the steering wheel rose up, larger than life in front of her face.

The sound of crunching bone accompanied a

shooting pain in Leah's head and the music finally stopped.

* * *

State Road 372
   North of Atlanta, Georgia
   Thursday, late afternoon

The cloying smell of copper roused Leah into consciousness. She blinked over and over, trying in vain to pull apart matted eyelashes. They wouldn't budge. Pain radiated from her shoulder and head and her whole body ached.

I have to clean myself up. I have to assess my injuries. The nurse in her operated on autopilot as she stretched over to the passenger seat to fumble with the glove compartment. It fell open and her fingers closed on a wad of napkins. With gentle pressure, Leah pried the worst of the sticky glop from her eyes and struggled to bring the car into focus.

The first thing she saw was the blood. It covered her shirt and pants and clung to her downy arm hair like a crumbling jacket. It was everywhere. *How am I still alive?* She patted her face with ginger fingers, easing up into her hair until a shock of pain made her gasp.

A laceration three to four inches long split her scalp just above her hairline and it still oozed with thick, clotting blood. Leah swallowed. *I need stitches.*

She twisted around in the driver's seat and found the seatbelt. It wouldn't open. She jerked on the belt and whacked the release with the base of her palm until at last it gave way. The entire back of her seat was warped toward the middle, with rips and tears in the fake leather. Stuffing leaked from the ruined back seat and fluffed in the breeze. Shattered glass littered the floor.

Leah turned to peer outside. The sun still shone, albeit lower in the sky. Was it the same day? Had she slept for thirty hours or only a handful?

Leah felt her neck for a pulse beneath a layer of crusted blood. Weak, but steady.

I have to get out of this car. I have to find supplies and close my head wound.

She turned to the driver's door and gripped it as a wave of vertigo and nausea roiled her stomach. She pulled on the door and handle and gave it a shove. The door wouldn't open. *Damn it.*

The crash warped the car so badly nothing worked. Leah swallowed down the bile in her mouth and crawled across the bench seat. Her duffel and air rifle somehow managed to stay put and Leah sent up a silent prayer of gratitude. At least she had some food and water and a weapon, no matter how meager.

She unzipped the bag and fished out a Gatorade. The citrus tang made her gag as the liquid hit her throat, but Leah forced it down. Blood loss meant dehydration and confusion. Hydration would be the key to staying alert and conscious.

The passenger door opened without issue and she

dragged herself out of the car and onto the asphalt. She didn't know where she was or which way to go. Her sister's house could still be twenty miles away. She was in a part of town she'd never been, bleeding from a head wound.

Helpless and hopeless.

She shook her head and the world spun. *I'm not hopeless. Not yet.* With shaky steps, Leah turned back to the car and grabbed the air rifle. She thought about Paul's instructions when he handed the gun to her outside the Walmart that morning: pump it a few times and then it's ready to fire.

Leah forced the pump action down and up. A wave of nausea passed and she pumped the rifle again. After six pumps, Leah sagged against the mangled frame of the car. It would have to be enough.

Her vision blurred as she picked up the duffel and slung it on her shoulder, but Leah didn't collapse. She gripped the car with one hand and the rifle with the other and looked around. No people anywhere. No one to ask for help.

Across the street, a boarded-up and abandoned strip mall stood like a silent sentry already prepared for the new world. Behind her, privacy fences led into residential backyards. A typical cut-through road on the outskirts of town.

She could go around to a house and knock on the door, but who would help her in this condition? She looked like a war zone survivor or a woman risen from the dead. And no house would have the supplies she needed: sutures and antiseptic and antibiotics.

Leah squinted into the distance at the only cross-street she could see. A sign sat on the side of the road, twenty feet closer than the stop sign. Leah forced her feet toward it.

As she closed the distance, her heart beat faster. She licked her lips and almost managed a trot. When the words became legible, Leah froze.

North Georgia Regional Hospital

An arrow pointed left. Despite the pain and vertigo and blood still coating her face and clinging to her hair, Leah smiled. A hospital would make everything better.

CHAPTER TWO

LEAH

Crabtree Parkway
    North of Atlanta, Georgia
    Thursday, late afternoon

The lyrics to the song playing before the crash echoed on repeat in Leah's head and she cursed at her own foolishness. Singing and speeding and pretending for a moment the world hadn't changed overnight? Mistakes like that could get her killed. This one almost did.

Trudging down the sidewalk, Leah blinked back the setting sun and willed her body not to collapse.

One foot in front of the other. That's all I have to do.

From the intermittent dizzy spells and the radiating pain deep into her skull, Leah surmised she earned a low-grade concussion to go along with the nasty gash. She needed to clean and treat her wounds and then rest and recuperate. All of which she could manage at a hospital.

The sign didn't proclaim the distance, but it couldn't be too far. Leah squinted into the sun. The orange orb hugged the line of houses and trees ahead. Sunset would be upon her soon. If she didn't find the hospital before dark, she would have no choice but to keep going. Stumbling around in the night wasn't the best option, but neither was passing out from blood loss.

The hospital would be running on generators and the dark might even ease her search.

She thought about her sister, Dawn, and her husband who hopefully waited in Hampton for her. Grant probably paced her sister's living room right now. His eyes would dart to the clock every five minutes. His fingers would wear a hole in his shirt as he rubbed it back and forth. He had to be worried sick.

If he couldn't sit still, he would be out there, somewhere, searching the streets for her. Leah needed to make it to Hampton. She needed her husband.

Everything that happened since the power went out filtered through Leah's mind. First the EMP and the twenty-hour shift in the hospital keeping babies alive and treating accident after accident. Then listening to her husband's frantic voicemails and leaving the hospital with Andy.

The explosion in the building across the street and the TV broadcaster warning of a nuclear bomb. Then the detonation. Blinding light. Risk of radiation exposure.

The long days and nights inside the bookstore.

A muffled sound pricked Leah's ears, but she ignored it. The trials of the past few days took up too much space to process anything else. The risky stop at the Walmart and the men who almost scared her to death.

A crack in the concrete caught Leah's toe and she stumbled. Her hand broke her fall as she landed half on the concrete and half on a strip of unruly grass.

"Get in here and fix this cooler!"

"Ain't no way I can fix it, Rhonda. It's broke!"

"Is not!"

"Is too!"

Leah blinked. The sound she had ignored was an argument. She scanned the street. A handful of houses in varying degrees of disrepair sat across the street. Not a single person on any porch. Leah scooted back into the grass of the yard behind her as the voices picked up again.

"If you don't fix it, I'm gonna throw it out in the street!"

Leah craned her neck to peer at the houses on her side. Maybe the couple arguing would help her. Maybe she could ask them for water and a clean towel to tend to her wound.

"You do that and the next thing you see'll be my fist in your face!"

Or maybe not. Leah scooted between two bushes, dragging her duffel along behind her. She couldn't risk being discovered. If the man yelling was willing to smack a woman around for throwing out a broken cooler, what would he do for a duffel full of Gatorade, power bars, and an air rifle?

Leah glanced down at the weapon. Paul said the air rifle wouldn't kill more than a squirrel or a rabbit, but a shot would still hurt like hell. If she had to, she could use it. She clutched the gun to her chest and eased further behind the shrub line.

The fighting couple traded insults, lobbing curse words back and forth like kids playing catch. Leah didn't know what to do. The longer the pair argued, the rowdier the insults became. The man shouted from somewhere outside, his voice rising with every word. Would they keep at it all afternoon?

Surely they would give up at some point. No one could fight forever. But what if it took hours? Maybe she should risk walking past or going around to a side street.

She shook her head. One look at her bloody face and clothes and a guy like that would see her as an easy target.

Leah brought her legs up underneath her. Waiting it out was the only solution. As she sat there, her eyes grew heavy. It didn't take much for the toll of the accident to catch up with her. She nodded off, the shouts and accusations no match for the weight of her eyelids.

"Meeooww."

Leah jerked awake.

"Meeooww."

A tabby cat paced back and forth in front of Leah's duffel bag, nose up in the air, sniffing. Leah reached for it, but it darted away.

"Meeooww."

"Shush. Be quiet."

The cat ignored her request and howled again.

"You hear that, Rhonda? I swear that cat of yours is

always getting into trouble! I told you to keep her in the house!"

"She won't stay. Every time I open the door, she runs right out. And I don't blame her!"

The cat yowled again and Leah shushed it. "If you don't be quiet, we're both going to be in trouble."

"If I find it, I'm gonna string it up on the back porch by its tail and watch it try to get out of that one."

"Howie Grunell, you will do no such thing." A screen door slammed. Feet thudded on a porch.

Leah reached for the cat. She scooped it up and ran a hand over its back. Its fur rumpled and a low rumble echoed from deep in its throat. "Shush, now. Just sit here and be quiet, and we'll both be all right."

The cat wriggled on her lap. Leah tried to hold it tighter. It arched and squirmed and the fur on its tail puffed up. As Leah tried to gain purchase, the cat twisted around and hissed in her face. Claws dug into her thighs and Leah gasped.

"All right. Where ya at? I'm comin' for ya."

Leah let go of the cat and it leapt straight for her face, hissing and clawing in an attempt to free itself. A paw connected with Leah's cheek and four claws drew blood. Leah fell back, a muffled cry all she could manage. The cat dove under the nearest branch and disappeared in a flurry of fur.

The slash marks on Leah's face burned and she brought her hand up to wipe at the fresh blood. Cats carried diseases. She needed to clean the wounds. At this rate, if she didn't get to the hospital and pump herself full of antibiotics, she was risking a lot more than a scar.

The bushes in front of Leah trembled and shook and the branches spread apart. A pair of dirty work boots appeared in the gap, followed by grease-stained jeans, a grubby T-shirt, and the face of a man who had too much liquor and time on his hands.

He smiled and a missing tooth pocked his grin. "Well what do you know. That damn cat might be useful after all."

CHAPTER THREE

GRANT

2078 Rose Valley Lane
  Smyrna, Georgia
  Thursday, 9:00 a.m.

Is that a baby? Grant rolled over, half expecting his wife to be lying there, cradling an infant they didn't have. Something cold and wet jabbed his cheek.

He jerked into consciousness.

A scrappy little mutt of a thing whined an inch from his ear and the horror of reality barreled into his brain like a runaway train. The EMP. The nuclear bombs. Millions of people dead.

His wife missing.

Grant scrubbed a hand down his face and sat up. It wasn't a dream or a bad memory he could shake with a cold shower and a hot cup of a coffee. The United States was about to fall apart, if it hadn't already.

Was the federal government functional? Did anyone even survive? Television shows made fun of secret presidential bunkers, but were they real? Grant didn't have a clue. For all he knew, the White House and the Capitol were smoldering craters in the ground with nothing but ash left to remember people by.

If all twenty-five bombs went off, were the rest of the states any better? Most of Georgia's government buildings were gone. With the legislature in session, that meant every representative and probably the governor, too. Who was left to call up the National Guard? Who could organize statewide relief efforts?

The dog whined again and Grant forced himself out of a sea of fear. The poor thing turned around in a circle on the bed and stared at him. "Need to go, huh?" Grant sighed and dragged himself off the bed.

Stumbling down the stairs, he escorted the dog to the back door. As he pulled it open, cold air contracted his pupils and sent a shiver straight to his bones. Without electricity, the frigid nights would be one hell of an issue. At least Atlanta didn't sink below freezing very often.

As soon as the dog rushed back past his legs for the relative warmth of the house, Grant shut the door. From the angle of the sun and the sound of birds chirping, it had to be mid-morning. He pinched the back of his neck and squinted into the dark kitchen. It still smelled like the dumpster outside his office when the trash service forgot to pick up.

Part of him had hoped against all odds that Leah would show up in the night. He'd dreamt of her slender but strong arms slipping around his waist. Her tender kisses full of longing and hope. But she didn't come home.

He didn't even know if she was still alive. Finding Leah was priority number one, but what if she came home while he was gone? One look at the slick of rotting liquid expanding into the hall and she would believe the worst. *No*. He couldn't leave without getting his house in order.

Leah needed somewhere safe to come home to. Somewhere they could try and survive together.

The dog sat bedside him, staring up with blue eyes full of hunger. Grant nodded at the dog. "Let's hit the kitchen, huh? There's got to be something still edible besides tuna."

After a single tail wag, the dog stood up. Grant reached down to pet it, but it shied away. He exhaled. "Sooner or later, you're gonna have to let me pet you or this deal is off."

He headed to the kitchen and stopped at the entrance. With daylight filtering in through the windows, the place didn't seem so bad. Black bananas on the counter. Moldy bread beside the stove. The refrigerator hid the worst of it. Grant reached under the sink and pulled out a trash bag and a pair of gloves.

Sucking in a deep breath, he opened the fridge door. The smell turned his stomach and Grant recoiled. He didn't even want to know what used to be in the vegetable drawer. After four trash bags and a morning of steady work, the fridge gleamed like the shiny stainless and plastic cabinet it had now become.

Never again would it keep a beer cold and a steak fresh. Grant set a still-good bag of oranges on the counter and shut the door. Besides the fruit, he'd managed to save three cans of Coke, an unopened box of chicken broth, and a container of baking soda. The rest was trash.

After mopping the floor, hauling out the trash, and sucking down a bottle of water, he opened another can of tuna for the dog and dumped it on top of a week-old takeout box of white rice. He toed the bowl toward the dog. "Beggars can't be choosers."

The dog snarfed it down in under a minute.

Grant scratched his stubble. He didn't want a dog. The furry thing was a complication in this new life. But he couldn't ignore it, either. Without Grant, it would struggle. With Grant, it might struggle less. And Grant had to admit, the company was a bonus.

He held out his hand and the dirty thing sniffed it before slinking away. "You need a bath, too. A good brushing and a bath." Grant smiled. "It'll happen. You watch."

The dog loped to the front door and sat with a view of the street, and Grant turned back to the kitchen. With the crackers, cereal, canned goods, and other odds and ends in his cabinets, he had enough food for maybe nine days if he stretched it thin. Half that if his wife came home.

Not nearly enough.

Grant closed his eyes. The house would provide

shelter. For now, the taps still ran. He could fill up the tubs upstairs and any containers or buckets. That left food and weapons.

He glanced at the dog still standing guard at the front door and took the stairs two at a time. After filling the tubs, he unlocked the safe in the closet and pulled out the only gun he owned, an M&P 9 Shield, and two full boxes of cartridges. 200 rounds.

While many of his former military friends subscribed to the basement-full-of-guns-and-ammo plan, Grant had always been a know-one-gun-and-know-it-well type of guy. But he'd also assumed the police would arrive with a single phone call and all Grant had to do was defend his home or person until they got there.

He hadn't planned on riding off into the Wild West or fighting for survival with no one to watch his back. It would take more than a pair of eight-round magazines and a couple boxes of ammo to build a stash and fortify his home.

Weapons and gas were his two biggest priorities, with food and water following right behind. Before he could set off in search of Leah, he would need to be prepared. Grant picked up the handgun and brought it into the bathroom.

Even a man on a mission could stop for a shower.

Half an hour later, with clean clothes and eyes wide awake from the icy water, Grant holstered the Shield and headed back downstairs. As he hit the last step, the dog's ears flattened and a low, menacing growl slipped from its throat.

Grant eased forward. The dog focused on something in the street. Grant stopped in front of the plantation shutters of his dining room and peered out. He didn't see anything.

The dog growled again.

Grant frowned. "Is it a person? An animal? I need more than a growl to go on, here."

The dog flattened down into a crouch and bared its teeth. Whatever was out there, the dog saw it as a threat. Grant checked his gun was safely tucked into his holster and pulled his shirt down to hide the grip.

He eased toward the door. "If I don't come back, the rest of the food is yours."

The dog glanced up at him, but didn't relax.

"Stay here." Grant unlocked the door and slipped out into the street.

The sound of screaming sent goosebumps across his skin.

CHAPTER FOUR

GRANT

Rose Valley Lane
Smyrna, Georgia
Thursday, 2:00 p.m.

Blood. Shouts. A man staggering in the street. It could have been the middle of a riot. A war zone after a bomb ripped the neighborhood apart.

But it was just Stan from three houses down, staggering like an extra from *The Walking Dead*. Grant eased off his porch and onto his driveway.

His neighbor, once young and fit and full of life, stumbled every other step. Bloody patches of his scalp showed where vibrant blond hair used to be. His chin dribbled with vomit and the sticky pale mess coated his shirt and stained his jeans.

A woman came running across the street, brown hair waving in the wind. Debbie, Stan's wife.

"Stan! Stop, you don't know where you're going!" She flailed her arms, struggling to catch up to her dying husband.

Stan collapsed to his knees and Debbie stuttered to a stop. She spun around, eyes wild and unfocused. "Help! Someone help us!" Tears streamed down her face. Exhaustion deepened the lines around her mouth.

Had she cared for him all this time? Did no one offer to help?

Grant swallowed back a wave of regret. No amount of care would help Stan now. Grant eased down the driveway, cognizant of doors opening and closing up and down the street. Shadows of onlookers, one after the other, appeared in his peripheral vision.

Jackie and Charlie.

Rebecca and John.

Kimberly, Steve, and their teenage sons Grant could never tell apart.

Every shout brought more and more neighbors. Gawkers and spectators, the lot of them. Grant strode forward, his arms outstretched.

Someone across the street shouted. "Stay back! It could be a virus!"

Grant shook his head.

"It could be Ebola! We could all die!"

Debbie spun around in a circle. "I'm not sick. If it were a virus, I would be sick!"

"It's not worth the risk!"

"Can anyone make a call? We need an ambulance!"

"There aren't any ambulances, you moron!"

Grant didn't try to place the voices with the people standing about. He focused on Debbie and Stan. The man heaved, hands on his thighs as he struggled to breathe. The bald patches on his head grew redder, swelling almost like tomatoes in the sun.

Part of Grant wanted to turn around and pretend he didn't see any of it, focus on finding Leah and moving forward. But the other part of him thought about his wife and her never-ending need to help others. It's what made her who she was; not just a good person, but a fantastic nurse. A woman willing to sacrifice her own health and welfare to keep someone else alive.

Grant knew what she would do. She would already be at Stan's side, comforting him and Debbie. Leah would help until Stan took his last breath.

I have to. For her. I can't watch Stan die.

Grant thought about the neighborhood parties where he clinked beer glasses with Stan and talked about the upcoming Braves' season and if it would finally be their year. The man didn't deserve to die on the street like a pariah with neighbors too afraid and weak to help.

None of them did.

Grant shoved his lingering doubt to the side and walked forward. He tuned out the shouts and warnings, all hollow and untrue. He held up a hand and shouted to no one in particular. "It's okay. I know what's going on."

He knelt beside Debbie and tried to smile. "Hey, there. Looks like you could use some help."

The woman's breath came in shallow bursts, in-in, out-out, seconds away from full-blown terror. Grant reached for her hand. He gripped it and squeezed. "It's okay, Debbie. I'm here and I'm listening."

She nodded between sobs.

"Try to calm yourself. Nice slow and deep breaths."

She struggled with his request, breathing in and out twenty times instead of one or two.

"You'll be no good to your husband if you can't breathe."

Debbie tried again, focusing on Stan's hunched-over form in the street. At last, she managed to suck in enough air to speak. "You shouldn't be here. We could be sick."

Grant smiled. "You said it yourself. If Stan had a contagious illness, you'd be sick already."

Debbie's brows knit together and she reached for her husband. When her hand touched his shoulder, he shuddered.

"How long has he been this way?"

"Since yesterday. He's been tired since he came home, and he said he had a headache, but I thought it was stress."

Grant counted back. The nuclear bomb detonated Saturday evening. Five days since the blast. From what the truckers shared while Grant waited out the radiation plume, a severe dose of radiation poisoning might take a few days to manifest. Moderate exposure would take even longer.

He swallowed. There was no easy way to ask what he needed to know. "Do you know about the bomb?"

Debbie nodded. "A few of us caught the news on

Eric's portable radio after the EMP. We didn't believe it was real until the blast."

"What was Stan doing when the bomb went off?"

She closed her eyes. "He was out for a drive."

Grant blinked. "His car still worked?"

"Motorcycle. It's a vintage Triumph. His pride and joy."

Grant nodded. "Do you know where he was?"

She shook her head. "But I know he saw the blast. He said he couldn't see very well because spots swam before his eyes, so he pulled over and waited until he thought it was safe enough to ride home."

Grant squeezed her hand. In an effort to stay safe, Stan poisoned himself. While his vision cleared, invisible particles of radiation landed on Stan's skin and clothes, killing him slowly. If he'd driven blind, he might not be dying in the middle of the street.

What a cruel way to go.

"Do you know what's wrong with him?"

"I think it's radiation sickness."

Debbie leaned back in shock. "From the bomb? But he wasn't downtown!"

Grant stared at Stan. The man couldn't speak or think or even make eye contact. He sat in a crumpled heap on the ground, bent over at the waist, clutching his middle. His head barely hung off the ground.

"The bomb vaporizes particles of debris and they get sent high up into the atmosphere. In the hour after the explosion, they fall back to earth, full of radiation. These tiny particles—so small you can't see them—land on your skin. If you get exposed to enough, it's lethal within an hour."

"And if you're not exposed to so much?"

"Then it kills you more slowly."

Debbie snorted back a wave of snot and tears and reached for her husband. This time he didn't even twitch. "Like Stan?"

"Yes, or even more drawn out. It could take weeks or months. But if you're exposed to a sufficient dose of radiation, it *will* kill you."

Her nostrils flared as she inhaled. "Am I going to get sick?"

"Were you outside?"

"No. But I hugged my husband when he came home. The second he walked in the door, I ran to him, clutching him tight." Her head jerked up and she stared with terrified eyes into Grant's own. "All the radiation on his clothes and skin. It must have gotten on me, too."

Grant forced his voice to stay even. He didn't know how his wife did this day after day. Caring for the sick and dying was one thing; dealing with their terrified relatives was another. He shook his head. "I don't know how long it lasts. But if you start to get any symptoms, then you'll know what it is."

"Is there a cure?"

"Not that I know of."

Debbie stroked her husband's back. "This is it, isn't it? This is the end?"

"For Stan?"

Debbie nodded, but didn't look up.

"I'm afraid so."

Her shoulders shook in a silent sob and she reached forward, draping her body over her husband's.

Grant turned away. He wished more than anything that Stan had stayed inside and gave Debbie a private moment to say goodbye. But maybe this was the best way. Now she knew the truth about his illness and her future.

If he hadn't been lucky enough to find the truck stop, Grant could be suffering the same fate. He could already be dead or in the throes of a sickness just like Stan. Was his wife suffering? Did she make it out of the blast's radius and find somewhere safe to hide?

He had to have faith that she did. He had to believe she would be coming home as soon as she was able. If he lost faith, what did he have to live for?

A wail rose up from beside him and Grant turned around in time to see Debbie clutching at her husband's face. His head hung limp and lifeless and his body sagged all the way to the ground. Stan was gone.

Debbie shook him, fingers digging into his stained shirt. "No! You can't leave me like this! You can't!"

Grant reached out and stopped her frantic arms. "He's gone, Debbie."

She blinked back another wave of tears. "He can't leave me here all alone. What am I going to do?"

Grant waited until she looked up. "You're going to keep living one day at a time. That's all anyone can do now." He eased closer to Stan and wedged his arm under the man's chest. "I'll carry him home."

Debbie nodded and stood up, waiting in the street

like a beggar woman while Grant hoisted her dead husband into his arms.

Stan weighed almost as much as Grant and he staggered before gaining his balance. They would need to bury him wherever Debbie saw fit, but for now, Grant just wanted the spectacle to end.

Neighbors from every nearby house lined the street. Women with hands covering their mouths, men looking away every time Grant made eye contact.

He adjusted Stan's lifeless body and followed Debbie to her front door. She let him inside and ushered him to the stairs.

"Can you put him on our bed? I can clean him easier up there."

Grant nodded and followed Debbie up the stairs. He laid Stan down on a bed with room for two and stood back. "I'm sorry, Debbie."

She pinned him with a fierce stare. "Thank you, Grant. For everything."

He nodded and stepped out of the room. As he descended the stairs, he couldn't help but see all the photos. Debbie and Stan on a cruise ship. The pair of them on the summit of some mountain halfway around the world. Their wedding photo.

On and on the photos went, showcasing their lives as an inseparable pair. What would Debbie do without him?

Grant stepped outside and shut the front door behind him. Everyone still stood where he left them, heads bent together in hushed conversation. A shout rang out from across the street. "What do you know?"

Pairs of terrified eyes peered at him from the faces of people he said hello to every day. People he called his friends. How many of them knew about the nuclear bombs? How many of them knew they were a country on the brink of either destruction or war?

Grant swallowed. One man thirty feet away could barely stand, he swayed on his feet, gripping the arm of his wife to stand upright. He was probably poisoned as well. How many others were just like him? How many weren't ever coming home?

"You said you know what's going on! Tell us."

"I heard it's a terrorist attack."

"I heard we've been invaded."

"Someone said we're all going to die. That there's some virus out there!"

Grant wasn't an emotional man. He'd managed to hold back the tears when his mom died from cancer when he was only eighteen and when his father passed of a heart attack years later. He didn't fall apart when Leah agreed to marry him or when he saw her that first time in her wedding dress.

But looking out at so many confused and scared faces, the gravity of it all hit him like a thunderbolt. These people didn't know what to do and they were looking to him for answers. For a solution.

He hesitated. *Should I stay or should I go?*

CHAPTER FIVE

LEAH

Crabtree Parkway
        North of Atlanta, Georgia
        Thursday, early evening

Leah swallowed down a thick glob of spit and snot clinging to the back of her throat. The man standing in front of her grinned like a farmer eyeing a prize tomato, red and ripe on the vine. Perfect for picking.

Her heart hammered in her chest and the higher her pulse, the worse the throbbing in her head wound. Panic would only complicate her injuries. *I have to stay calm. I have to keep a clear head.* Leah thought of herself as a patient in the ER and forced her breathing to stay even.

The man nodded at her head. "Pretty nasty gash you got there."

Leah didn't know what to do. If she nodded and

joined in the conversation, would he take it was a sign of weakness or just general politeness? She opted to stay on the ground and not say a word.

He frowned. "Not much of a talker, are ya? We can fix that. How 'bout ya come on out so I can get a look at ya."

Leah pressed her lips together. Paul and the other men at the Walmart had terrified her until she realized they were only there to protect the place. What if this man were the same? She could be turning down an offer to help or offending someone for no good reason. But the more he leered at her, the more the hair on the back of Leah's neck stood on end.

Stubble coated his jaw in a scrappy, hit-or-miss beard, and the smell coming off his breath mixed liquor and coffee in a noxious combination that spoke of late nights and later mornings. From the wrinkled T-shirt and the stained jeans, Leah guessed the man hadn't gone to work or taken a shower for days. Maybe even since the power went out.

Did he know about the nuclear bomb? Was he already hungry and desperate? If Leah asked him some questions, he might be able to tell her what life had been like the last six days that she'd been apart from society. From the nonstop action of the hospital to the days trapped in the bookstore, she didn't know what was happening out in the rest of the world.

He rubbed his chin and tucked his brow. "You gonna come out or what?"

Leah pulled the air rifle tighter to her chest and slid back further across the grass.

The man chuckled and shook his head. "I ain't seen one a those since I was a kid. Whatcha gonna do? Shoot my eye out?"

"I don't want to." Leah's voice came out scratchy and raw from lack of use. "I just want to be left alone."

He snorted. "That ain't much fun at all. 'Sides, ya look like ya need some help."

"I can manage."

"Howie, ya out there? What the hell's takin' so long? You get lost lookin' for that cat?"

"Can it, Rhonda! I'm busy!" Howie turned back to Leah with disgust curling his lip. "That old lady a mine can't never leave it alone. Always *Howie this*, and *Howie that*. A man can't get no peace round here."

He took a step forward and lowered into a crouch so his eyes met Leah's on the level. "I'm only gonna ask one more time. Come on out here onto the sidewalk. I won't hurt ya."

Leah risked a quick glance behind her. Either the people living in the house whose lawn she crouched on weren't home, or they weren't coming to her aid. If she shouted, Leah doubted anyone would care; they'd been listening to Howie and the Rhonda woman go at it for goodness knows how long.

Running would get her nowhere fast. She didn't know the area and if she veered off course, how would she ever find the hospital? Leah gripped the rifle tight and came to a decision. She would play along. For now.

At last, she nodded. "Give me some room."

Howie stepped back with a flourish.

Leah clambered to her feet. The duffel thumped against her back and sent waves of pain through her muscles. She would have to check for serious bruises, too.

As Howie moved through the bushes, Leah followed until she stood on the sidewalk. The last few inches of sun warmed her face and she held up her free hand to shield her eyes from the light. "If you don't mind, I need to go before it gets any darker."

"Where ya headed?" Howie stood on the sidewalk, shifting his weight back and forth.

Leah couldn't read his expression with the sun casting shadows across his skin. Was he nervous? Excited? Bored? She had no idea.

"Grocery store." Leah lied out of instinct. "Looking for some medicine to clean my cut."

"Ain't gonna find one that's open. Everything's been shut down since the power went out."

"Can't hurt to try."

Howie stepped forward and his nostrils flared. "Where you been, lady, under a rock? Ain't nothin' nowhere that's gonna help you. It's all closed up. Stores, gas stations, even the damn hospital's dark."

Leah swallowed. "It is?"

He scratched at his neck and glanced past Leah toward what must have been his house. "Tried to get my wife to go a few days ago. She ain't been feelin' right since that big light in the sky."

Leah covered her shock with a cough. Didn't they know what happened? "What light?"

"You know, that big flash that lasted forever. Gave me spots all across my eyes for days."

She played along. "I was stuck at work on a double shift. With no power, we had to do everything by hand."

He jabbed a fingernail in his mouth and chewed on it. "You really didn't see it? Dave from down the way tried to tell me it was some sorta bomb, but he's always been a nutter."

"Who the hell you talkin' to out there?"

Leah twisted in time to see a woman ease down a set of worn wood steps on a front porch three houses away. She stopped a few feet from Leah and palmed her hips. In the gloom, Leah could make out what looked like scabs on her arms. Burn marks? Radiation? Leah couldn't be sure.

"Get back inside, Rhonda. I'm busy."

"I can see that. Ain't you gonna introduce me?"

Howie frowned and pointed a finger at Leah. "Don't know her name. Found her in the bushes tryin' to hide."

"Whatcha hidin' for?" Rhonda almost spit. "Ain't like Howie's gonna hurt ya. He couldn't do nothin' even if he tried."

"Aw, don't go spoutin' off now, woman. You know that ain't true. Show her the lump I gave you for talkin' back last week."

Rhonda crossed her arms. "Don't know what you're talkin' about."

Howie caught Leah's eye and pointed at his wife. "I

can't get no respect around here. Not even from my own wife. Can you believe that?"

"Seems like she has a point."

Howie closed the distance between them. "What'd you say?"

Leah stepped back and added her free hand to the rifle's grip. "It seems to me you're not very nice."

"Who are you to call my Howie not nice!" Rhonda stormed up from the other side and stopped close enough for Leah to get a look at her. Bloodshot eyes, broken capillaries on her nose and cheeks.

"Have you been sick to your stomach? Throwing up?"

Rhonda snorted. "What's it to you?"

"Were you outside when the bright light hit?"

Rhonda glanced over Leah's head to her husband in alarm. "What's she talkin' 'bout, Howie?"

"Hell if I know. Whatever you've got to say, spit it out."

Leah's gaze bounced between Howie on the one side of her and Rhonda on the other. She knew she should keep her mouth shut for her own safety, but if the woman was sick, Leah might be able to help. She could at least explain the signs of radiation sickness and how to alleviate the symptoms.

She cleared her throat and forced a tight smile. "The light you saw the other day was from an explosion. A nuclear bomb."

Howie shook his head. "No freakin' way. Here in the States? Not possible."

"It's true. Bombs went off all over the country. As many as twenty-five. If your wife is throwing up and feeling dizzy and tired, it's probably low-grade radiation sickness."

"That's crazy talk. Why should we listen to you? That gash on your head's probably makin' you hallucinate."

"No. It's not." Leah focused on Rhonda. The woman had fallen silent as soon as Leah began to explain. "Were you outside that day?"

Rhonda nodded, her fingers, trailing over her lips. "I was at a friend's house. We stood on the back porch and watched the whole thing."

"That don't mean nothin'."

"It means she needs to rest and take care of herself and monitor her symptoms." Leah focused on Rhonda. "If your hair starts falling out, or your skin thins and starts bleeding, you need to find a working hospital."

Howie exploded. "I told ya, the damn hospital's shut down! My Rhonda's not sick. She's just fine."

"I've been throwin' up for two days, Howie. I ain't fine."

"She needs some medical care. If you show me to your house, I can clean myself up and check her out."

"You? Why should I trust someone covered in blood?"

Leah straightened up. "I'm a nurse. I can help."

Howie's eyes narrowed. "You ain't helpin' her. She's not sick."

"She could die."

"Rhonda's gonna be fine."

Leah opened her mouth to argue when Howie's fist came out of nowhere. It slammed into the same cheek cut from the cat and Leah stumbled backward.

"She's gonna be fine!" Howie screamed again and charged.

CHAPTER SIX
LEAH

Crabtree Parkway
  North of Atlanta, Georgia
  Thursday, early evening

Leah landed smack on her backside in the dirt between the bushes. The leaves whooshed back into place as if she'd fallen through to another dimension. Her ears rang from the blow to her head, compounding her concussion and scrambling her senses.

She scuttled back on the grass, digging her heels into the ground as the bushes shook and parted with Howie's rage. How did everything turn so wrong, so fast? One second, she offered to help his wife, and the next she was fleeing from a madman.

Leah huffed out a rebuff. "Leave me alone!"

"My wife isn't sick! You're gonna pay for what you said!"

"I didn't do anything to you!"

"She's not sick!" Howie lunged for Leah and she kicked out at him, missing his face by an inch.

He swiped at her with an open palm and connected with her ankle. His fingers wrapped around it and Leah swung the air rifle up toward his face.

"Let me go!"

Howie snarled and Leah did the only thing she could think of. She pulled the trigger. A pellet discharged from the gun and hit Howie square in the cheek. He howled and let go of her ankle, grabbing at his face as blood welled in the pocked wound.

Leah scrambled to her feet. She pumped the gun once, but Howie reared up before she could pump again. He lunged for her, blood covering his hands and face, arms outstretched like a zombie in a horror film.

Spinning around, the duffel bounced against Leah's lower back as she took off through the side yard of the two nearest houses. Howie followed a few steps behind, cursing and spitting and shouting at her to stop.

Leah didn't know where she was or where she was going, only that she had to move. Gaining distance between her and the crazy man on her heels was the only option. She tried to pump the rifle again, but couldn't gain leverage as she ran. It was as good as a cudgel, but nothing more.

Curtains in a side window moved against the glass and Leah slowed, hoping someone would come for her. Howie shouted and the fabric fell back into place. No one would help her with that man chasing her down.

The side yards opened to a quad of fenceless backyards with strips of grass and sunbaked concrete. Leah ran through them and onto the next street with Howie still behind her. Darting to her right, she sneaked between another set of houses and past short fences and a little yapping dog.

Leah shouted into the air. "Help! Someone help me!"

No doors opened. No windows rattled. No one was coming to her aid. Tears leaked from the corners of her eyes as she risked a glance behind her. Howie was no more than twenty feet away, intent on chasing her down. How would she ever get away?

With every pounding footfall, her tears loosened bits of dried blood and dirt from her lashes and it stung her eyes as she ran. Dizziness washed over Leah in waves and she stumbled as a curb rose up in front of her.

One hand hit the ground, but she shoved herself upright, plowing on down another street and past more and more houses. She couldn't process anything but movement. She could be headed north or south or around in circles. It didn't matter as long as Howie didn't catch her.

Air sawed in and out of her mouth as she struggled for enough oxygen. She couldn't keep this up forever. Sooner or later he'd catch her or she'd collapse. A set of bushes ten feet high loomed up ahead and Leah ran for them, darting behind the screen as Howie screamed from the street.

"You won't be able to get away from me!"

Leah ducked behind the house and kept going,

refusing to look back. Three houses away a detached garage sat tucked into a back corner of a lot and Leah raced for it, hugging close to the houses where no fences blocked her way. As she slipped into the open garage door, Howie's shout echoed from the opposite direction.

"I'll get you one way or another!"

When she'd ducked behind the bushes, he must have kept to the road, hoping to cut her off at the pass. *If I hadn't stopped, he'd have me.* Leah shuddered as she crept around a cold four-door sedan. A stack of plastic tubs in the back gave just enough cover for her body and Leah crammed down between them, shoving her duffel beside her.

Leah took the rifle in two hands and pumped. It was loud, but she had to take the chance. She pumped four more times and exhaled. If he found her, she would defend herself.

Howie's taunt stuck in her head. If he found her, she'd aim for his eyes.

The cold concrete beneath her soaked through her scrubs and into her muscles. Everything either throbbed or ached or lanced with pain. From her head to feet to shoulders, Leah was at the end of her stamina. The longer she sat there, panting and slowing her heart, the more the rush of adrenaline gave way to an exhausted crash.

She wanted nothing more than to fall asleep right there on the dirty cobweb-covered floor and sleep for days. Maybe when she woke up this would all be a nightmare and she would be home in her bed with her husband by her side.

A noise startled her still. *Oh, no. Please have it not be Howie. Please let me catch a break.*

The top of the tub in front of her shifted. The dirty blanket was alive. It stretched and stood up and pinned Leah with a pair of yellow eyes.

She bit back a groan. Of all the creatures to be sleeping in a garage. It had to be a cat. Leah frowned at it and managed a hoarse whisper. "If you start meowing, so help me God, I'll shoot you."

The cat flicked its tail, turned around in a circle, and lay back down.

Leah exhaled.

With every passing minute, the garage grew darker and her hiding place increased in value. By the time the sun disappeared, Howie would never be able to spot her in the back. Leah knew she should leave. The cover of darkness was the best time to escape his frantic, unhinged searching.

But Leah couldn't stand even if she wanted to. The car crash and the terror of the chase sapped all her energy. Asking her to walk out of there was like asking a marathon runner who just finished a race to do it again, only this time faster.

Leah closed her eyes. She would sleep it off and figure it out in the morning.

* * *

"*Psst.* Here, Snowball. Here, kitty, kitty."

Leah blinked her eyes open. Darkness still surrounded her. She couldn't have been asleep for more than an hour or two.

A can rattled with something dry and crunchy inside. "Come on, Snowball, come get your dinner." An old woman's voice accompanied the shaking can.

Leah froze. A bent-over shape stood in the open garage door, one hand on a cane, the other holding what looked like a metal coffee can.

The cat on the tubs rose up in a stretch, curving its back as it yawned.

"That's it old man, come on inside. I know it's not the wet food you like, but it's better than nothing."

The cat jumped down from the tubs and paused to rub its head across Leah's sneaker. She clenched her teeth and eased the barrel of the rifle off her shoulder.

"Would you like to come in, too?"

Leah jerked her head up in alarm, but stayed silent.

"I can't promise a hot dinner, but I've got more than dry cat food inside."

Is she talking to me? Leah glanced around, but in the dark, she couldn't see anything. Had the woman spotted her while she'd slept? Would this be the start to another Howie chase?

Leah chastised herself for falling asleep in a stranger's garage. *I should have escaped while I had the chance.*

The woman sighed. "I'm not going to stand out here all day. The damp air makes my bones ache."

Leah cleared her throat. "A-Are you talking to me?"

"Well, I'm not talking to the dust bunnies, that's for sure."

Leah lifted the rifle.

The old woman chortled. "Put that thing away. Howard's gone home."

"The man chasing me? How do you know?"

"Because I watched that wife of his drag him back across the street by his ear. That's why. Now get off that dirty floor and come in. You could use the break and I could use the company." Leah opened her mouth to argue, but the old woman waved her off. "I'm not taking no for an answer."

"Seems to be the common tactic around here."

"Well, mine won't come with a side of drunken idiot. Follow me if you so choose." The old woman turned toward the front of the garage and stepped out.

Leah watched for a few paces before hauling herself up to stand. She winced. While the cold ground numbed her muscles, it did nothing to ease the pain. She needed the warmth of a house and medical treatment.

An elderly woman wouldn't pose too much of a threat. As she hobbled to catch up, the cat slinked into the waiting open door ahead.

CHAPTER SEVEN

GRANT

Rose Valley Lane
   Smyrna, Georgia
   Thursday, 4:00 p.m.

Grant exhaled. So many faces stared out at him from positions on the sidewalk. Friends and neighbors, some he knew and some he didn't recognize. A few children clung to their parents in terrified little bundles, cueing off the fear pounding in everyone's hearts.

How many of them knew about the EMP and the following nuclear explosions? How many of his neighbors had worked through what that would mean for the future?

The gravity of the situation buffeted Grant like hurricane-force winds.

The United States as everyone knew it was gone. No more red and blue states or talking heads on TV stirring up imagined grievances. No more infrastructure or endless supplies. Every major city was dealt a death blow, not just to their epicenters, but to their entire way of life. How many major businesses had headquarters in the heart of cities? How many could function if their heads were cut off?

Had New York been hit in the heart of the financial district? If so, goodbye Stock Exchange, lifetime savings, all of it. Without power to the East Coast or anyone left alive in financial centers to bring banking back, the country would grind to a halt.

Even if banks opened, they would run out of paper money and how long would it be good for? Once people figured out store-bought food was a finite resource, US currency would be worthless. So many people scrimped and saved and worked their entire lives to prepare for an orderly future. What would they do now as everything slipped into chaos?

Grant ran a hand through his hair and brought his thoughts back to a local scale. Without shipping companies trucking in food daily, even if grocery stores opened, they wouldn't stay open for long. People would be hungry. Neighbors would be pitted against neighbors and friends against friends.

Families would struggle to survive. Would the police forces still operational cease to function? How could anyone ask those brave men and women to come to work when their families back home went hungry?

Cities would dive into anarchy.

He thought about the riots that broke out every time

an unpopular news story hit the press. Was it the same now? Was midtown Atlanta in the midst of a riot? Were the parts of Chicago and New York and Los Angeles that survived the nuclear blast rife with mayhem?

It was only a matter of time.

Hunger turned people desperate. Cold made them bold. Two weeks or a month from now, how many of the faces staring at him like he could wave his hand and make everything better would still be alive? How long before society completely fell apart?

Part of him wanted more than anything to turn and run. Grab a backpack and his bits of food and get out of the city before anyone tried to take what little he had. But he couldn't leave without Leah. If she was out there, somewhere, she would be coming home. He couldn't leave until he either found her dead body or she ran into his open arms.

As long as he stayed in his house, he would need to help his neighbors. Leah would never forgive him if he boarded up the door and sat with his gun in his lap, daring anyone to come near. She would expect him to help. To have grace and kindness and charity.

And in his heart, Grant knew it was the right choice. Until someone forced his hand and made it impossible to stay, he would be a good man and a good husband and lend his support to the community.

Most of his neighbors had no idea how hard the coming days, weeks, and months would be. Even Grant didn't know, but together, maybe they could find a way to persevere. Maybe his neighborhood would join together and create their own little town. One more welcoming and accepting than Hampton turned out to be.

Grant cleared his throat and held up his hands. "If anyone wants to talk about what's happened this past week and what we can do to help each other going forward, I propose we call a neighborhood meeting." He glanced at his watch. "How about six o'clock tonight at the neighborhood clubhouse? We can share all we know and together we can come up with a plan."

A handful of neighbors in the crowd voiced agreement, others nodded and hurried their children back to their homes. Doors opened, people walked off in groups of two and three, and Grant took a deep, fortifying breath.

He would share his knowledge and offer any advice or assistance he could, but it didn't mean he wouldn't protect himself. Even if the neighborhood rallied together, Grant would fortify his house and protect against those who wanted to shortcut their way to survival. It wasn't that different than his IT job when he thought about it.

He awarded hackers who found flaws in his company's software, then he forwarded the information and the coders fixed the errors. What was that saying? *The best defense was a good offense.* He wasn't going to sit around and wait for someone to come to him. He would prepare as best he knew how.

Grant strode back to his house with purpose. As he opened the door, a little wagging tail and patient eyes greeted him. He bent down with his hand and held it out.

The dog hesitated, but didn't run away. Grant reached for under its chin.

His fingers slipped through the dirty fur and the dog didn't move. Grant gave it a few scratches before standing up. "See? That wasn't so bad. Pretty soon, you'll be begging me for a bath. I know it."

The dog trotted over to the back door and Grant let it out. Ever since the dog hopped into the Cutlass, Grant had refused to think of a name. He'd even refused to acknowledge the obvious. But as he watched the tenacious little thing relieve itself in the yard, he had to face it: she was his and she needed a name.

"Soon. I'll pick one soon." As the dog hurried back inside, Grant got to work. With an hour before the meeting, he had enough time to rig up a few defenses. First, he hauled the four sheets of plywood he never got around to installing as flooring in the attic out of the garage, along with his tool box.

The plantation shutters on the first floor facing the street were great for keeping out prying eyes, but they did nothing to keep determined people out of his house. Grant ensured the shutters were closed before nailing one sheet to the bottom half of the double window and one to the top. He left about a two-inch gap at eye level. With the inset of the shutters, he could still open the slats and peer out, but it would take a hell of a lot of work to break in.

Plywood wouldn't stop a bullet, but it would slow down a burglar.

He used the remaining two sheets on a pair of

windows in his home office just off the kitchen, boarding them up without a gap. The back of the house sported enough windows that he could afford to forego the visibility of two.

After another trip to the garage, Grant managed to fix a scrap piece of fiberboard to the small window in the laundry room and create an under-the-doorknob security bar. Shoved beneath the front doorknob, it would buy Grant a few minutes of time if someone tried to break the door in.

Four windows and a door remained unsecured on the back of the house. Grant palmed his hips and thought it over. He could rip the plywood he'd installed last year in the attic down and make a permanent fix, but he couldn't manage that in the next twenty minutes. That would be a project to tackle in the daylight when he could not only see what he was doing, but he could take his time.

Too much noise might attract the wrong types of neighbors. He didn't want anyone to know he'd already begun to secure the place. He didn't want anyone to think his trust was already gone. And it wasn't; not entirely. But he'd learned in his IT job that no one could truly be trusted. Ordinary people did crazy things when they thought no one was looking or they wouldn't be caught.

Turning to the kitchen, Grant rummaged around in the junk drawer until he found the two combination locks he'd kept around for the gym membership he'd been meaning to renew. They wouldn't keep out a determined thief, but they could keep a less-resourceful neighbor from sneaking into the backyard.

Grant hustled outside and locked the gates on either side of his house before checking the time. Almost six. Whether he liked it or not, the house would have to remain partially insecure.

He hurried inside, wiped a sheen of sweat off his brow, and chugged one of the sodas he'd saved from the fridge. The dog sat by her empty bowl, but Grant only smiled in apology. "I'll go on a scouting mission soon, I promise. But for now, it's one meal a day, I'm afraid."

As if she understood, the poor little thing trotted over to the front door and curled up by the sidelight Grant had left exposed. He would figure out a way to cover it as well, but with the doorstopper in place, it didn't worry him tonight.

He opened the door and bent down to dog's eye level. "Keep watch, will you? Anyone comes near and you let them have it." Grant shut the door and half-jogged to the clubhouse. He couldn't be late to his own meeting.

CHAPTER EIGHT

GRANT

Neighborhood Clubhouse
   Smyrna, Georgia
   Thursday, 6:oo p.m.

The clubhouse teemed with people. Grant hadn't seen so many of his neighbors in one place since someone organized a block party last summer complete with a keg and dollar hot dogs. He shoved his hands in his pockets as he leaned against the wall to keep from fidgeting.

Tons of people crammed in a little room didn't bother him, but in a minute or two they would all be looking at him for answers. He made it a point to see the show, not be the show, in his day job. It had been a mantra he'd stuck to for his entire life. Now he'd inadvertently jammed himself front and center.

As the top of the hour passed, the room grew quiet.

Pocket conversations died down and a gaggle of eyes turned toward Grant. He swallowed. *Now or never.*

He propped up a smile. "Thanks for coming, everyone. I know watching Stan collapse in the street was tough."

"Do you know what happened to him?" Dan, a retired grandfather who lived one street over spoke up. "Looked like he'd been sick all over the place."

Grant nodded. "Stan had been out riding his motorcycle when the bomb went off. He died of radiation poisoning."

A muted gasp rolled through the crowd. A voice Grant couldn't place rose above the murmur. "Do we know for a fact it was a bomb? I heard someone say it was an explosion."

"By all accounts, it was a nuclear bomb."

"Couldn't it have been an accident? Like a power plant meltdown or something?"

Oliver, a young guy who was new to the neighborhood, spoke up. "It was a coordinated attack. Not just here, but all across the United States. Didn't you see the news?"

"How?" Dan scoffed. "Our power's been out since Friday!"

"Just because you don't have power, doesn't mean you can't access the world. Radio and television stations were still broadcasting all over the West Coast. And the internet's still there. All of Europe and the rest of the world are still online."

"How are you accessing it?"

"Up until yesterday, via my personal hot spot that was pinging off a satellite internet connection. But it's been too cloudy for my solar panels to get a decent charge."

Grant motioned for Oliver to join him at the front of the room. "Sounds like your knowledge far exceeds my own. Care to share?"

The twenty-something shrugged. "I guess, but I can't tell you the accuracy of what I've seen. You all know the reliability of the internet."

"I'm sure everyone here understands that."

A chorus of agreement echoed and died as Grant's neighbors waited for a report of the information they used to access at their fingertips.

Oliver cleared his throat. "It appears at least twenty major metropolitan areas were hit with a coordinated, timed attack. Nuclear bombs, all about the size of the one dropped on Hiroshima, were detonated in key business and city centers between five and six Saturday night."

"It can't be true." A woman sitting on the floor in front of the clubhouse couch shook her head. "That would kill millions!"

"The initial explosions leveled multiple city blocks. In New York there were reports of massive rolling aftershocks that toppled most of Manhattan. The entire financial district was destroyed."

Grant closed his eyes. It was as bad as he feared. Maybe worse. "What about DC?"

"I never saw confirmation it was hit."

"So it could be all right?"

"Or it could be razed to the ground. DC is only ten miles wide. The whole thing could be irradiated rubble."

"What are we going to do? Who's going to help us? We need the power back on!" The same woman in the front row almost sobbed.

Grant spoke up. "We need to be prepared for the worst-case scenario. With so much destruction and radiation over the hub of Atlanta, the power may be impossible to restore."

Another man nodded. "The grid was hit before the nuclear bombs detonated on the ground. I saw that on my phone Friday night. The mini cell tower by my office had a generator. I was able to get online for a few minutes before the network was overloaded."

"Why would someone do that?" Another woman squeezed between two men on the couch stared at him in disbelief.

"It's an act of war; do you really need an explanation?"

Another neighbor across the room voiced her concerns. "Are we under attack? Where's the military? Why isn't anyone saying anything?"

"How exactly would they do that? Our entire state government was vaporized. If DC was hit too, then there *is* no government." Oliver shook his head. "This isn't like us storming the beaches at Normandy. This is country-ending."

"The military wasn't hit. Can't they mobilize? Aren't they on the way?"

Dan chimed in. "If what these men are saying is true,

then no, they won't be on the way. The army doesn't have standing orders on what to do when the US goes to hell in a nanosecond."

Grant waded into the rising terror. "We need to band together as a community. If anyone else is experiencing symptoms like Stan, we can offer aid."

"Isn't radiation poisoning fatal? If anyone's sick, won't they die?"

"It depends on the dose. If you weren't exposed for very long, you may just suffer burns or gastrointestinal distress. You can recover."

"Is it contagious?"

"No."

"Are you sure that's what killed Stan?" Jennifer from across the street spoke up for the first time. "What if there were chemical attacks, too?"

"It was classic radiation sickness. It had all the signs."

"How do you know? Are you a doctor?"

Grant shook his head. "No, but my wife's a nurse and I read all about it after the detonations." He wasn't about to tell anyone that Leah wasn't home or that he learned about it from a trucker on the state line. "We're not at risk of contagion."

"I still think we should be careful." Jennifer wrapped a sweater tighter around her shoulders and glanced up at her husband. So far, he hadn't offered his opinion. She turned back to Grant. "Do you really think the power's out for good?"

"I don't know. But without any operational city infrastructure, I wouldn't expect it back anytime soon."

Dan agreed. "Last time we had that ice storm it took, what? A week for the power to come back? With a nuclear bomb, we're as good as in the Stone Age." He snorted. "Better get used to candlelight."

"What are we going to do without power?" The woman on the floor almost swooned. "Everything in our house is electric."

Grant rubbed his cheek. "There're a few things everyone can do now to prepare. The water's still running, so you should go home and fill all your bathtubs and any containers you can find. When the pumps fail, we might never have running water again."

Jennifer closed her eyes and leaned against her husband. "What about food? Without power will any stores even open?"

"Clean out your fridges and freezers if you haven't already and inventory your supplies. If you don't have a sizable pantry, you'll need to ration."

A chorus of shouts broke out from all over the room.

"We're almost out of everything!"

"All my food was in the fridge and it's ruined!"

"My daughter's allergic to so much, we shop a couple times a week. How are we going to get what she needs?"

"What about pharmacies? I'm diabetic and I need insulin."

Grant held up a hand. "I'm afraid I can't answer any of your questions, but that's why we're all here. We can rally together and help everyone in the neighborhood."

Kimberly from the corner house on Grant's street emerged from the crowd. "We should share our food.

Everyone should bring what they have here and we can split it up."

"Are you crazy? What if someone has a ton? They just have to give it away? They paid for that food."

She turned around to try and identify the voice. "Would you rather your neighbors starve?"

Harriet from two houses away leaned into her husband and whispered a little too loud. "She probably doesn't have any food left. Look at how skinny she is."

Grant tried to step into the melee. "I don't think we need to start confiscating food just yet. But we could assemble some teams. One to check on all the neighbors who didn't come tonight. One to scout nearby stores for food and supplies. A neighborhood watch would be good, too."

"Why do we need that?"

Dan crossed his arms. "Who else is gonna take care of us? The police? You really think city police are gonna go to work when they ain't gettin' paid?"

Jennifer tapped her husband on the arm and the pair of them squeezed through the crowd for the door. A few other couples and singles followed. The neighborhood was not coming together like Grant hoped. Maybe it was the shock of the news or the cacophony of thoughts pinging in people's heads, but the silent departures rattled Grant.

They couldn't survive as a community if they weren't willing to hear everyone out.

He raised his hand for attention. The conversations simmered, but didn't completely quiet. "How about we regroup tomorrow after everyone has had a chance to digest the news?"

At his quasi-conclusion, the clubhouse erupted into conversations. The woman on the floor stood up on shaky legs and almost collapsed until Barry from the first house in the neighborhood grabbed her under the arm. Other people fled as quickly as they could without starting a stampede.

Dan and a single woman Grant knew in passing made their way to the front of the room. They greeted Oliver and Grant with nods.

"It's Susie, right?"

The woman nodded. "I'm at 2260, all the way down the street from you." She shook Grant's hand. "Thank you for setting this up. I know people like to shoot the messenger, so it was brave to stand up here and take it."

Grant shifted on his feet and felt the familiar heft of his Shield in his appendix holster. "It was the least I could do."

Dan glanced at the retreating crowd. "So what the hell do we do now?"

Grant smiled. "I've got a few ideas."

CHAPTER NINE

LEAH

57 Parrot Lane
    North of Atlanta, Georgia
    Thursday, 9:47 p.m.

Leah squinted as she stepped into the squat brick bungalow.

"Lord have mercy. Did Howie do that to you?"

"Do what?"

The woman waved a frail hand in Leah's general direction. "Cover you in all that blood."

"Car crash." Leah reached up to her head, but stopped midway. "I was headed to the hospital when that guy's cat wouldn't leave me alone."

"Figures. That cat's always over here trying to poop in my azaleas. Won't leave unless I sic a broom on him."

Leah smiled and the cuts on her face lanced with pain. "Is there a place I can clean up?"

"Bathroom is the second door on the left down the hall. There are towels in the cabinet and a lantern on the back of the toilet. You're welcome to run a bath."

"Thank you." Leah stepped out of the kitchen and found the bathroom down a wallpapered hallway covered with dated photographs of years gone by. She stepped into the little room, turned on the lantern, and shut the door. Her back hit the wood and she sucked in a breath.

I'm safe. Howie can't get me here.

She closed her eyes and concentrated on her breathing. In and out, slower and slower, until the last bit of adrenaline spurring her on faded. She would be no good as a nurse to herself if she couldn't stay calm and focused.

After another deep breath, Leah pushed off the door and confronted her face in the mirror. What she saw would terrify anyone. Dried blood cracked across her cheeks and matted her blonde hair into sticky clumps. A set of four gashes spread from above her left eyebrow to her chin, already puckering with fresh scabs.

Between the blood and the dirt and the snags from running through bushes, her top was ruined. At some point, she would have to go home for more clothes. But she needed to make it to Hampton first. It's what her husband begged her to do.

Leah stripped out of the ruined shirt and the rest of her clothes and turned on the water in the tub. The bathroom looked original to the house with a rose-pink porcelain sink and matching tub. Pink and yellow tiles alternated along the wall. Classic 1950s, full of hope and promise.

As soon as the tub filled, she eased down into the icy water and dunked her head. Pain shot through the wound, but the freezing temperature kept the worst at bay.

She couldn't risk a shower. The fragility of her scalp foreclosed any chance of a nice shower spray. If she damaged the skin, she may not be able to suture it closed once she finally reached the hospital.

With gentle exploration, Leah cleaned the blood from her body and face and finally her scalp. The water turned from clear to gray to rust as she cleaned the worst of her wounds. As she stepped from the water, a surge of emotions wobbled her knees. Leah gripped the edge of the sink and watched droplets of water run down her legs.

I could have died.

The memory of the crash hit like the impact all over again and she sagged onto the toilet seat. She survived an EMP and a nuclear explosion only to almost die through her own stupidity. If she hadn't escaped from Howie, would he have killed her? Would she have died on some street she didn't know without ever seeing her family again?

Leah choked on her own spit and hubris, coughing into the sink until her ribs ached from the effort.

"You okay in there, honey?" The old woman's voice carried through the door.

She stammered a response. "Y-Yes, I'm fine. I'll be out in a minute."

"Good, because these biscuits won't eat themselves."

Biscuits? Leah reached for her bag with a frown. *Did she really say biscuits?* If the woman were senile, she didn't know what she would do. Smile and leave as soon as possible, she supposed.

After dragging on her clothes with care, Leah rinsed the tub and hung the used towel. So much kindness from a stranger. She would need to repay the woman somehow. Maybe she could gather some supplies at the hospital and bring them back. A first aid kit and some medicine or even some food would be helpful.

Leah opened the door and the smell of hot bread popped her eyes wide open. She trundled into the kitchen with her duffel and mouth wide open. "You really made biscuits?"

The old woman turned around with a smile. "Of course. No one comes to Tilly Orion's house without eating." She pointed at the small wood table. "Put your things down and sit. You'll need to eat before we tend to that head wound."

Leah did as she was told, tucking her duffel beneath the table before easing into an empty chair. A collection of items sat in front of her: a sewing kit, a package of rolled gauze, and a bottle of gin. She smiled at the gesture, but she wouldn't be patching herself up in a non-sterile kitchen. She tucked her hands in her lap. "Tilly is it?"

The woman nodded as she slid a tray of steaming biscuits into a bowl and held them out.

"I'm Leah Walton." She took the biscuits and set them on the table. "It's nice to meet you."

"Pleasure's all mine, dear. Butter with your biscuits? I've still got a bit left."

"Sure."

Tilly reached for a covered butter dish and brought it to the table. "Tea will be ready soon, too. Just waiting for the whistle."

Leah nodded. "Do you mind if I ask how you managed to cook?"

"Stove's gas and it's still running same as the water. Don't know how long it'll hold out, but I figure as long as I've got flour and water I can cook up some quick bread. After that, it'll be cold cans of green beans and marmalade I suppose."

Tilly held up the bowl and Leah plucked a single biscuit from the steaming pile. She buttered it and took a bite, relishing in the hot, flaky goodness. "This is amazing. Thank you."

"No trouble."

The tea kettle piped up and Tilly pushed herself up to stand. She leaned on her cane as she walked the handful of steps back to the stove to shut off the burner. "Hope you don't mind Lipton. It's all I've got."

"I'll drink week-old sludge as long as it's hot."

Tilly chuckled. "My old Roger used to like his coffee so thick you could eat it with a spoon." She grimaced as she wobbled the kettle back over. "I never could drink the stuff."

Leah held out an empty mug and Tilly filled it. "Is it just you here?"

"Roger died a few years ago. Now it's me and Snowball. You two already met out in the garage."

Leah nodded. How long would a woman like Tilly make it without resources? Leah took a moment to really examine the woman. Gray hair piled up on her head. Velour track suit with worn elbows. Giant eyeglasses that magnified a pair of deep-set brown eyes. She could have been anywhere between a rough sixty-five and a spry ninety.

Whatever her age, Tilly seemed to handle the lack of power like it was no big deal. It could have been any other day forty years ago on a farm with a local girl stopping in to gossip the day away.

The oil lamp on the table lit the entire kitchen, and with the hot buttered biscuits, Leah almost forgot the horror of the past few days. Only the throbbing in her head kept the past in focus.

"Do you know how far away the hospital is from here? I need to get there as soon as possible."

Tilly blew on her tea before taking a sip. "It's about two miles, give or take, but no sense in going there."

"Why not?"

"It's closed."

Leah sloshed her mug and winced as a drop of tea singed her hand. "What do you mean it's closed? Even if it's at capacity, the emergency room should be triaging patients."

"They can't. There's no power."

"What about the backup generators?"

Tilly shook her head. "Either it doesn't have any or they aren't working. My neighbor Jill walked there the day before yesterday to ask about asthma medication for her daughter. She said it was hopeless. There were signs all over saying they were closed due to the power loss."

Leah focused on her tea. Part of her wanted to rise up and blame the hospital for turning people away, but she'd made the same decision. When she thought her life was at risk and her husband needed her, she left. She walked out of Georgia Memorial and left everyone behind to die in a nuclear explosion.

She couldn't cast stones at a hospital administration that decided to close when she made the choice to leave. But without a working hospital, what would she do? How would she treat her injuries?

The bottle of gin still sat on the table and Leah glanced up at Tilly. Now it all made sense. Like it or not, an old woman's kitchen would have to do. "You don't by any chance have fishing line in that sewing kit, do you?"

Tilly smiled and the wrinkles around her eyes deepened until she looked like an owl. "I've got invisible polyester thread. It's as good as fishing line and a bit more resilient, too."

Leah exhaled. "How about shot glasses?"

"They're just above the sink in the glass cabinet."

"Good. I'm going to need a drink."

CHAPTER TEN

LEAH

57 Parrot Lane
   North of Atlanta, Georgia
   Friday, 12:30 a.m.

"I can do this by myself if you need to sleep. It's the middle of the night."

"No, dear. The older I get, the less sleep I need. Some days I wonder if I'm a vampire, then I remember I don't even like rare steak."

Leah picked up the shot glass brimming with clear gin and braced herself. "Here goes." She tipped her head back and swallowed the burn of alcohol. It filled her nose like a hit of turpentine and she gagged. "How do you drink that stuff?"

"Usually with a glass full of ice, but the ice maker's on the fritz."

Leah laughed out loud and the tension in her muscles eased. She squared her shoulders. "I can do this."

"Yes, you can." Tilly picked up a handheld mirror and wedged it between a makeshift stand of books. "Is this good?"

Leah peered at her reflection and the gaping wound. "It'll do."

After eating as many biscuits as she could stand, she had small-talked with Tilly until the older woman reminded her the gash on her scalp wasn't closing itself. Now it was time to work.

She inhaled and opened the sewing kit. A pair of scissors rested on top of rows of thread and Leah pulled them out. After a wipe of gin across the blades, she hacked at her hair, cutting as close as she could to the wound without risking more injury. Once the wound was free of stray hairs and she could get a closeup look in the mirror, Leah assessed the damage.

Three and a half inches long, mostly straight without too many jagged chunks. Although she learned stitching in nursing school, Georgia Memorial required doctors to perform any sutures. Leah hadn't stitched a real person in years. But inspecting the wound gave her courage. *I can sew this. It's not that different from hemming a pair of jeans.*

She rolled her lips over her teeth and picked out a sturdy needle.

What I'd give for a sterile suture kit right now. At less than a dollar a pop, they were something she kept in her expanded medical kit at home, but she'd given Grant her travel bag when he started commuting longer distances to work and she never had time to make a second bag for herself.

Add it to the list of things she failed to do before the end of the world: no pre-determined rendezvous point, no packed bag ready to get her home, no spare battery charger lurking in the bottom of her duffel. All of her failures in preparation paraded through her head as she threaded the needle with the clear polyester thread.

She should have made a get-home bag like FEMA suggested. Then she would be prepared to handle anything that came her way with good shoes and spare clothes and emergency rations. Instead, she was leaning on the charity of a woman twice her age and a sewing kit assembled before she was born.

Leah knotted the end of the thread and gave it a yank. It stretched more than suture thread, but held. She'd have to make the stitches neat and tight.

With a calming breath, she doused the needle in the gin and brought it up to her scalp. *The first is always the worst.* She thought back to the little girl in the hospital thrashing around on the bed at the sight of a needle. Was she alive now? Did she make it out of the blast zone in time?

The needle pierced her scalp and Leah let out a cry. Pain shot through her skin and deep into the connecting muscle. She pushed her wound together and whipped the first stitch.

"That's it, honey. You're doing just fine."

Leah glanced at Tilly over the mirror. "If I pass out, can you tie off the suture wherever I leave off?"

The old woman nodded and Leah brought her attention back to the mirror and her own pale face. A wave of nausea roiled her stomach, but she fought it back. *I can do this.* She inhaled through her nose and ground her teeth together before diving back in for the second stitch. It hurt as bad as the first, if not more.

On and on she worked, no longer taking a break between stitches, but pushing on through the never-ending pain until the last bit of the wound closed. She tied the thread off and clipped it with the scissors before falling back in the chair.

Sweat beaded on her brow and Leah shivered. The job was done, but she would need medicine to prevent infection.

"Have another drink. It'll bring the color back to your cheeks."

Leah nodded as Tilly poured a shaky shot. "Is this how you got used to gin?" She downed the liquor as Tilly smiled.

"It happened to be the cheapest liquor in the little bodega around the corner from our apartment when my husband and I were first married. When you're scrimping on a custodian's salary in Brooklyn, you drink whatever's shoved down on the bottom shelf."

"You're from Brooklyn?"

"Born and raised. Didn't come down here until my husband retired. We were sick of the snow."

Leah turned toward the hall where family photos lined the wall. "Any other family?"

Tilly glanced at the table as she recapped the gin. "My son is in Manhattan. He's a banker. Or... At least he was. I can't imagine he survived the blast."

"So you heard?"

"My neighbor was closer to town when the bomb went off. He came over and told me all about it."

"I'm sorry about your son."

"It's okay, dear. We all have to go sometime."

Leah stared at the old woman. "How are you going to get by here all alone?"

Tilly waved her off. "I might not be as mobile as I used to be, but I've got a full pantry, plenty of toilet paper, and a double barrel shotgun under the bed." The fluffy white cat from the garage interrupted with a soft meow and Tilly bent down to pat its head. "And Snowball here's a good judge of character."

Staying to help Tilly wasn't possible; neither was bringing her along to Hampton. But Leah hated the thought of using her supplies, accepting her sanctuary, and offering nothing in return.

"How about you? Do you have someone waiting on you somewhere?"

Leah nodded. "My husband and sister are up in Hampton. I need to get there as soon as possible. I just have to find a way to get there without a car or a good sense of direction. I'm not the most reliable judge of which way to go."

She rubbed her lips as she thought of the time she

drove all the way to Macon before she realized she went the wrong way on I-75. Grant didn't let her live that down for years.

Grant.

The thought of her husband sent a pang of longing through her. She needed to get home.

Tilly stood with a grunt and motioned toward the living room. "Take your things and make yourself comfortable on the couch. I can bring you a blanket."

"No, I should be going. I don't want to take any more of your time."

"Nonsense. You need sleep. If you set off now, all you'll do is run into some more trouble. It's better to rest and make a fresh start in the morning."

Leah's brow pinched. "Are you sure you don't mind?"

"Not one bit."

She exhaled. Tilly was right. No matter how much she wanted to set off now, how would she even pick the right direction in the night? If she collapsed on the street, Howie could find her. She needed to sleep and rebuild her strength.

While Tilly plodded down the hall, Leah focused on the present, cleaning up her mess in the kitchen. Now she owed the older woman even more for her troubles. There would have to be a way she could return the favor.

"Here we go." Tilly set a pillow and a blanket on the couch and turned off the oil lamp. Darkness flooded the bungalow, but after a few moments, the light from the moon and stars cast enough of a glow to see.

"Thank you again. I don't know how I can ever repay you for this kindness."

"Just enjoying your company is enough for me. Goodnight, dear."

"Goodnight." Leah watched Tilly's bent form disappear down the hall before easing down to the couch. Exhaustion tugged at her eyelids and she could barely mange to slip off her shoes before falling over onto the cushions. A few hours of sleep and she would leave. Hampton was still a long way away and without a car, Leah had no idea how long it would take to get there.

She drifted out of consciousness with a frown creasing her healing scratches.

* * *

An incessant banging filtered through Leah's skull and at first she thought it was her throbbing wound.

"Hold your dang horses. I'm coming."

As Tilly's voice pierced the fog, Leah blinked into the morning.

A fist whammed on the front door and Leah sat up. The whole room spun. Had Howie from the night before found her? Was he there to finish what he started?

She smacked her dry lips together and managed to speak. "Who is it?"

Tilly eased up to the door and peered through the peep hole. She pulled away with a frown. "Neil from next door and he looks like hell."

Leah exhaled. "Is he dangerous?"

"Only to mosquitos. He's a pest-control technician." Tilly unlocked the door. "Now what on earth has you all up in a tizzy, Neil?"

A man with bloodshot eyes and hair sticking up in all directions rushed into the house. "It's Mary. She's sick. I don't know what to do."

Leah perked up. Finally something she could handle. "I'm a nurse. Can I help?"

CHAPTER ELEVEN

GRANT

Neighborhood Clubhouse
 Smyrna, Georgia
 Thursday, 8:oo p.m.

Oliver walked over to the clubhouse door and peered out through the top glass. "Everyone sure left in a hurry."

"A lot of people were in denial these last few days." Susie perched on the arm of the sofa and tightened the bun at the base of her neck. Grant pegged her for late forties or early fifties. Wearing a pair of Merrell sandals and hiking pants, she already had the perfect wardrobe to survive the end of the world.

Susie dropped her hands and turned toward the window, peering out at the darkness of the street. "I hope the meeting woke a few of them up."

"How many houses are in the neighborhood?" Dan

scratched at his graying hair above his ear. "Eighty? A hundred?"

"Eighty-seven, if I remember right. I still have the brochure on the neighborhood somewhere from when I bought my house." Oliver rejoined the group with a frown.

Combined, they were four out of eighty-seven households. If the rest weren't willing to stick it out and figure out how to get by, they didn't have great odds. "What happened around here after the attack?"

"At first?" Dan glanced up at the ceiling, trying to remember. "Everyone just thought it was a power outage. I sure did."

"I was still at work. Friday nights, the campus bookstore is open late." Susie tucked a stray strand of brown hair behind her ear. From the Georgia Tech shirt she wore, Grant guessed she worked at the two-story bookstore in midtown. "My car didn't start when I tried to leave, so that was my first clue. I snagged a ride from a coworker who drives a classic Mustang and it took us ten hours to get here." She snorted and shook her head. "He told me to never ask him for a ride again."

Grant nodded. Reaching Atlanta from Charlotte wasn't a walk in the park. "What about Saturday before the blast?"

"Everyone was business as usual. People were running errands. A few gas stations had working generators and the Publix up the road was open for cash purchases."

"They were even taking checks." Dan flashed a

rueful smile. "Don't carry much spare change on me these days."

Oliver spoke up. "I caught a lot of news coverage from the West Coast Friday night. Even then, people were saying it was a terrorist attack and that more might be coming. There were some rumors about bombs, but no one believed them. They thought it was ISIS or some other group blowing smoke."

Dan perked up. "Did anyone say who did it?"

"No." Oliver shook his head. "It was all conjecture."

"Any chance you can pick up some news stations now?"

"I doubt it. Even if I get eight solid hours of sunshine tomorrow to charge my solar panels, it's been harder and harder to get a connection every day." Oliver pushed his glasses higher up his nose. "Satellite internet is all I've been able to access, but even then it's hit or miss."

"What about DSL?" Dan lifted his eyebrows in hope. "That's over the phone line. Does it even need power?"

"It's down. I'm pretty sure the EMP torched the central offices. I think they have backup batteries for a while, but we're at almost a week. Nothing can stay online that long without power."

Dan sank down to rest his large frame on the arm of the couch. "So it's hopeless?"

Oliver hedged. "The satellite connection isn't great, but I was able to access a few websites earlier in the week. It really depends on where the satellite company's connections are routed and their congestion. The EMP might have thrown them off track, too."

Grant exhaled. They couldn't sit around and do nothing waiting for confirmation of what they already knew. America was in chaos. Cities would be in turmoil, with looting and fires and people dying from radiation sickness. Country towns would be grappling with a future without power.

Not many people were as resourceful as Oliver. Grant never thought to keep a solar charger at home or have a means to access the internet if his Wi-Fi didn't work.

He'd checked his internet connection in between cleaning the mess in the kitchen, but he'd known it would be hopeless. Without the electrical grid, he'd never get cable internet or cell service. He hadn't thought to check the regular phone line. "Even the copper phone line needs the grid?"

Oliver nodded. "The central offices are giant switchboards. It's the same as it used to be with operators answering the phone and plugging lines in on a grid in front of them, it's just a computer doing the heavy lifting."

"Without power, that means we're cut off."

"Essentially, yes."

Grant straightened up as he remembered the truck stop. "Not entirely. If we can get access to a ham radio, we can connect with some folks. I waited out the radiation plume at a truck stop on the state line. They've got a network of radio operators all across the country. If we rig one up, we can communicate."

"That's a fine idea." Excitement lifted Dan's voice. "I

used to tinker with a ham when I was a kid. There's a local store not far from here that sells radio equipment. If it's open, we can see what we can pick up."

Grant nodded. If the shop hadn't been looted, they might have a chance. He didn't know how to set up a ham, but with Dan and Oliver they could figure it out. Information wouldn't change their day-to-day predicament, but it would help reality set in for the rest of the neighborhood. Hearing about the bombs would bring home the gravity of their position.

He glanced at each of his three neighbors in turn. "Do you all have any supplies to tide you over? Food, water, weapons?"

Dan hoisted up his belt and faded jeans. "I don't have much food, but I've got a couple of hunting rifles and a bunch of ammo."

Susie covered her neck with her hand. "Do you really think weapons are necessary?"

Grant nodded. "If not now, then soon. Even if our neighborhood stays peaceful, outsiders will come and we can't guarantee they'll be friendly."

"You mean thieves?"

"You've seen riots on the news."

Dan let out a breath. "What about Hurricane Katrina? Without necessities, desperation sets in quick. It makes people do crazy things."

Susie balked. "It hasn't even been a week. No one's desperate yet."

"Give it a month." Oliver ran a hand through his short

black hair. "I spent a summer helping local farmers in South America. A major coffee supplier convinced them all to convert their subsistence farms to coffee plantations."

He swallowed and glanced at the floor. "They cut down shade trees and wrecked the natural habitat to install full-sun coffee orchards. It killed the soil and the ecosystem they'd relied on for decades for their basic food needs. When they didn't get the yield the corporation wanted, it pulled out and left the farmers to fend for themselves."

"That's terrible." Susie frowned at Oliver's story. "What happened to the farmers?"

"Nothing good. When you're hungry, you'll do things you never thought possible." Oliver looked up with cold sincerity. "Don't discount what's coming."

Susie tore her gaze away. "If we need supplies, how do we get them? Nothing is open."

Grant spoke up. "We'll need to scout. Start with the surrounding area. Sometimes places don't look open, but there's still an owner inside willing to work with good people. I gassed up the Cutlass at a closed gas station thanks to just such a situation."

He left out the part about disarming a would-be robber.

"Then we should start first thing in the morning." Dan straightened up. "I can dust off my hunting gear and hand out some rifles. I haven't used them in years, but it's like riding a bike, ain't it?"

"I don't know the first thing about guns." Susie

worked her hands back and forth in her lap. "I probably can't shoot the siding off a barn."

"I don't, either." Oliver shrugged. "Never had the opportunity living in the city."

Grant pressed his lips together. Of the four of them, he was the only reliable shot. Not the best odds. "In all likelihood, we won't have to use them. Just having a weapon and making it known should be enough to ward off any trouble."

"Where should we go?"

"Gas stations first. I need gas for the Cutlass in case we can't find anywhere local for supplies."

"There's a sporting goods store about a mile down the road. I say we go there after we get gas."

Dan nodded. "The radio shop is on the way. We could hit it on the return."

Grant flashed a tight smile. "Sounds like a plan. How about we meet up outside my house at nine tomorrow morning? It'll give us plenty of daylight so we know what's coming."

Everyone nodded and the group broke up.

Oliver opened the front door and they filed out one at a time. Almost every house sat black and quiet. Here and there, small candles flickered in windows.

Susie broke the silence. "What do you think everyone else is doing right now?"

Grant sucked in a breath. "Waiting."

"For what?"

"Someone to help them." Grant parted ways with the group and headed toward his house. Halfway there, a barking dog quickened his steps. He might not have named her yet, but he could tell her voice apart from the other dogs in the neighborhood.

Grant hurried up the driveway and unlocked the door. The little dog darted out and rushed to the Cutlass. She ran around it, whining and sniffing. Grant bent to inspect the car and let out a curse.

The car sagged against the ground, its whitewall tires deflated and empty. Someone slashed all four. The dog stopped circling and stood beside him, ears pricked and alert.

"Guess I struck a nerve, huh?" He reached out and scratched the dog beneath the chin and she didn't back away. "Not much I can do about it now. Let's go in and rustle up something to eat."

She scampered inside and turned back to wait for him. Grant smiled. He really needed to come up with a name.

CHAPTER TWELVE

GRANT

2078 Rose Valley Lane
    Smyrna, Georgia
    Friday, 7:00 a.m.

Grant hauled the ripped-up plywood down from the attic
before the sun made a dent on the darkness. While the
dog curled up on the couch in the living room, he
boarded up the remaining windows in the back of the
house and fashioned another door bar out of two strips of
plywood nailed together.

All that remained were the two exposed sidelights on
either side of the front door. He couldn't leave them
open. Anyone could walk up to the window and get a full
view of the inside of his house. But he couldn't slap
plywood on them either. Then everyone would know
he'd at least prepared for the worst even if he hoped for
better.

He palmed his hips and exhaled. A bed sheet with plywood backing would have to do. Taking the stairs two at a time, he hustled to the linen closet and pulled out a spare pair of sheets for his bed. Leah had picked them out a year ago and made sure Grant never washed them on too hot a setting so the fibers didn't break down.

With a snip of his scissors and a hefty pull, Grant ripped the top sheet into strips. Leah would have to understand. If the neighborhood deteriorated as quickly as Grant feared, she'd be thankful for the privacy. Grant tacked up the sheets like curtains in the windows before measuring the last plywood board.

He cut it down to size with a hand saw and a fair share of sweat before nailing the strips on top of the windows. When he finished, Grant stood back to assess. Every window was covered. Every exterior door sported a bar beneath it to prevent kick-ins.

Assuming the dog stayed alert and on patrol, the house was as safe at it could be without being obvious.

A knock on the door startled him and Grant loped up to the peephole. He pulled it open with a smile. "Hey, Dan."

"Morning." The older man stepped inside and wrinkled his nose. "Doing some early-morning carpentry?"

Grant shrugged. "Can't be too careful."

Dan glanced at the plywood on the windows. "Last I checked, nuclear bombs don't create zombies."

"No, but they do make for a bunch of hungry

neighbors." Oliver's stomach rumbled as he two-timed it inside. "Spoke to Susie this morning. She's not coming."

"Is she sick?"

"Afraid, mostly. Can't wrap her head around the guns, I think."

Grant nodded. He could understand the fear. People who didn't know how to shoot or understand firearm safety had a tendency to overreact. "How about you? Does the thought of holding a gun freak you out?"

Oliver pushed his glasses up his nose. "Not really. I can't say I know what I'm doing, but I've played my fair share of first-person shooter games. Can't be all that different."

Dan snorted out a laugh. "If you say so." He held up two rifles. "I could only clean two of them to the point where I think they're a sure thing. I've got two more at home, but they're a bit rusty. I was afraid they'd jam."

"Then two it is." Grant used the hem of his shirt to wipe off his forehead and ushered the men into the kitchen. His 9mm and the shotgun sat on the counter. "I was going to give Susie the shotgun, but since she's not here, I'll leave it. I'm a better shot with the Shield."

"What's our plan?"

Grant washed his hands and holstered his handgun. "Thanks to some charming neighbor last night, my car is out of commission."

Oliver's face fell. "What happened?"

"Slashed all the tires. Took me the better part of an hour to wheel it into the garage and out of sight. That thing's a beast."

"Any idea who did it?"

"None." Grant glanced at the dog still sleeping on the couch. "But she'll probably let me know if they come around again."

Dan leaned over to catch a glimpse. "Since when did you get a dog?"

"She hopped in the Cutlass when I was on the way home."

"Does she have a name?"

"Not yet."

"Looks like a Stormy to me."

Grant thought it over. Good, but not quite right. "I'll think of something." He turned his attention to the trip ahead. "Now that we're on foot, we'll have to be strategic. We can't carry too many supplies. So I think we shift our focus to a sporting goods store as the priority. We can buy some packs and other supplies and huff them back home."

"What about food or weapons?"

"We'll have to see what they have."

"What if they aren't open?"

Grant shrugged. "We'll bridge that gap when we come to it."

Dan nodded. "Let's get on with it. We should aim to get back before dark."

Grant took one last look at the dog on the couch. "We'll be back in a few hours. Keep the peace."

She looked up at him as if in confirmation, watching as the three men walked toward the door.

* * *

An hour later, Grant eased down behind a half-height concrete wall. Dan scooted behind him and Oliver wedged in to his left. Fifty yards ahead, the road opened into a four-way intersection with a gas station on the closest corner.

They had made an agreement to head straight to the sporting goods store, but something about the area ahead gave Grant pause. He squinted into the distance. From their vantage point, he could make out plywood covering the windows and a spray-painted scrawl across the front door of the gas station's mini-mart.

"Can either of you read that?"

Oliver leaned closer. "No Gas. No Food."

"Why are we stopping?"

Grant held out a hand. "Can I borrow your rifle?"

Dan handed over the rifle with the scope and Grant perched it on top of the wall. He adjusted the view and scanned the gas station. He pulled it down with a ragged exhale. "Something about this station didn't feel right. Then I saw that lump. It's not trash."

"What is it?" Oliver rose up to look, but Grant held out his other arm.

Dan took the rifle and exclaimed a moment later. "I'll be damned. It's a dead body."

"Are you serious? Let me see." Oliver took the rifle and looked through the scope. A minute later, he set it in his lap and turned a pale face toward Grant. "He's been shot. There's a pool of blood all around him."

Grant nodded. "Looks that way."

"We have to go home. If there's someone out here shooting, we're easy targets."

Grant held up a hand. "Don't panic yet."

"Why not?"

"We don't know the circumstances. It could be the guy tried to break in. Maybe someone who works there is inside, guarding the place."

"And maybe there's a sniper on the roof waiting to pick the next group of idiots off."

Dan nodded. "The kid's right. If we're going to reach the sporting goods store, we need to keep a lower profile. Stick to the side streets or the backs of the buildings."

"It'll make the trek a lot longer."

"Do you want to get yourself killed?"

Grant exhaled. He hated to admit it, but his companions were right. The last thing they needed was a run-in before they even reached their destination. He pointed toward the closest side street. "If we head that way, it's mostly residential. We can skirt the main drag, using backyards or quiet streets and make it in an hour."

Oliver stood up and hustled down the alley, skirting a closed nail salon on one side and a photo studio on the other. Grant and Dan followed a handful of steps behind. They emerged into a neighborhood of twenty-year-old homes, built with large two-story walk-ups and postage stamp front yards.

Grant puffed out his chest. "Let's walk like we're patrolling the neighborhood."

"What if someone confronts us?"

"We tell them the truth: we're headed into town to check things out."

"But we don't live here."

"Doesn't mean we can't give them a little security."

Oliver chewed on his lip. "I say we do what you said before and sneak through yards."

"And give someone a reason to shoot us out their back window?" Dan shook his head. "No way. Grant's right. Let's own this."

Oliver grumbled under his breath, but kept stride with Grant and Dan as they paraded down the middle of the quiet street. Three blocks in, a woman tended to weeds in her front flower bed.

Grant nodded her way. "Ma'am."

She nodded back, eyebrows raised.

Oliver leaned over once they passed out of earshot. "She's still staring at us."

"But she's not shooting. Keep walking."

Forty-five minutes later, they emerged at the back of a strip mall. The sporting goods store sat sandwiched between a pet store and an office supply store right in the heart of the business district.

Grant jogged to the corner of the building and took a quick a look at the front parking lot. Half a dozen stalled cars littered the lot, but he didn't spot a single person. He hustled back to Dan and Oliver. "It's a ghost town. No one's here."

Oliver deflated. "This was all a waste of time."

Grant pinched the back of his neck and looked over

at Dan. The older man stared back, echoing Grant's internal dilemma.

"Seems a shame to go home empty-handed."

"But we can't get in. They're closed."

"We can get in if we want to." Grant glanced at the loading dock sitting quiet and empty twenty feet away.

"You mean break in? Like a bunch of thieves?"

Dan chuckled. "I was thinking more like men on a mission, but, yeah."

Grant added his own thoughts. "We can pay for everything we take."

Oliver shook his head. "I don't know."

"You can wait out here."

After a moment, Oliver shook his head. "No. You're right. We need supplies."

"Then we're breaking in?"

Oliver offered a pained smile. "More like inviting ourselves, but yeah."

Grant nodded and walked toward the back door.

CHAPTER THIRTEEN

LEAH

57 Parrot Lane
 North of Atlanta, Georgia
 Friday, 8:00 a.m.

Leah stood up and stuck out her hand. "Leah Walton. Pleased to meet you."

Tilly's neighbor stood in the doorway, unease pulling his bushy eyebrows together. He managed a brief nod. "Neil Unders."

Leah dropped her hand.

Neil scowled at Tilly. "Who is she?"

"Just what she said. She's a nurse."

Neil dropped his voice and leaned closer to Tilly. "But how do you know her?"

Leah spoke up. "She doesn't. I was in a car accident yesterday and Tilly graciously offered to let me stay here while I patched myself back up."

Neil motioned to her head wound. "That's how you got that?"

"It is. I stitched it up here last night, thanks to your neighbor's kindness."

He frowned. "I just came looking for some aspirin. Mary can't keep anything down and her head is killing her. I thought maybe if she could get rid of the headache, she'd be able to eat."

"How long has she been sick?"

Neil glanced at Tilly before answering. "Four days."

"Was she exposed to the blast?"

He ran a hand over his stuck-up hair and puffed out a breath. "Really, now. I appreciate your interest, but I don't have any idea who you are."

"Oh, for goodness' sake, Neil." Tilly used her cane as a giant pointer and waved it in Leah's direction. "She's a nurse. What does it matter that I can't announce her full pedigree? Let the woman take a look at Mary. If she's sick, Leah can help."

He didn't answer.

"I can't promise I can help, but I can at least offer some ideas as to what's causing the sickness." Leah tried to maintain an open and honest expression. It wasn't the first time she'd talked to a reluctant family member. "I know I must look a bit frightening, but I'm lucid and good at my job."

Neil ran his tongue over his lips. "You stitched up your head all by yourself?"

"With nothing but my handheld mirror and sewing

kit, Neil." Tilly leaned on her cane with a smile. "She's the real deal."

His shoulders sagged in defeat. "All right. You can come."

"Good man." Tilly nodded at them both. "I'll be here waiting."

Leah followed Neil out the front door and across the driveway to the house on the right. Like Tilly's, it occupied a small footprint on the lot, with a planter box running the length of the front porch and a picture window in front of the driveway.

Neil opened the door and ushered Leah into a cozy living room with barely enough room for a couch and a TV. He eased the door shut and locked it before turning around. "My son is still sleeping, so if we could be quiet, I would appreciate it."

"Of course." Leah followed him down a hall to a half-open bedroom door.

Neil pushed it open and Leah caught sight of a woman almost in a fetal position on a queen-sized bed. "Honey? I've got someone here to see you."

The woman shifted, lifting her head off the pillow and scanning the doorway with clouded eyes.

Leah stepped forward. "Ma'am? I'm Leah Walton. I'm a nurse and your husband gave me the okay to check you out."

The woman smacked her cracked lips together. "Mary Unders." She eased a hand underneath her side in an effort to sit up, but Leah waved her off.

"Don't go to any trouble. I can check you out lying

down." Leah stepped closer to the bed as Mary sagged back onto the mattress.

From the smell of dried sweat and stale vomit, Leah could tell she had been bedridden for a while. "When did your symptoms start?"

"A few days ago. They've been getting worse every day."

"Your husband said you have a headache and nausea? Trouble eating?"

Mary tried to swallow and coughed on her own spit. "Every time I move my head, it's like a thousand hammers set to work on my skull."

Leah leaned closer. Faint traces of pink skin on the woman's scalp showed signs of exposure to radiation. A scab on her arm could have been a burn. "Have you had any spontaneous bleeding? From the nose or eyes?"

"No."

"What about diarrhea?"

"Just vomiting."

"Have you been able to keep anything down?"

"Not for a day, at least."

Leah eased down into a perch on the edge of the bed. "What about fevers? Any chills or shakes?"

"No."

She exhaled. "I'm going to need you to think back a few days." Leah glanced at Neil, who stood with his arms crossed in the doorway. "If you can add any details, please."

He nodded.

"Do you all know about the bomb?"

Neil nodded again. "Mary saw the blast."

Leah figured as much. She turned back to the sick woman. "Where were you?"

"On the east side of the city. I work part-time at a private school teaching an advanced composition class. I was in my office that day trying to figure out how to lesson plan without power when the blast lit up the sky."

"How did you get home?"

She smiled until her cracked lips caused a split. "I bike to work every day. It's my only real exercise."

"Mary used to be a long-distance competition cyclist. She could have done the Tour de France."

"Could not."

"Could, too."

Leah smiled at the pair of them arguing. She could feel the love radiating between them. It made her job all that much harder. She turned back to Mary. "I believe you're suffering from radiation sickness. The plume of radiation must have tracked eastward as it fell back to earth."

"Am I going to die?"

"I don't know."

Neil huffed behind her, but Leah plowed on. "But a few things can help. An IV for starters. Since you can't keep anything down, you're dehydrated. If we can get some fluids in you, then your body will be better equipped to ride out the sickness."

"Where are we going to get an IV?" Neil's voice rose despite his sleeping kid. "You couldn't even go to the hospital for stitches. How can we ever hope for an IV?"

Mary struggled to pull herself off the pillow. "Neil, can I talk to Leah for a moment? Alone?"

He frowned. "I don't see why."

"Please."

"I'll be in the living room." He turned on his heel and almost stormed down the hall.

Mary fell back onto the bed and sloughed off a breath. "So how bad is it, really?"

Leah swallowed. "Since I don't know how much radiation you were exposed to, I honestly don't know. But you know you're sick and I think you're worse than you've been letting on."

"I left as soon as the blast faded. I had to be out there for two hours, breathing hard and really exerting myself. I wanted to get home."

Leah didn't say anything.

Mary struggled to swallow. "Every day is worse than the last. I can tell by the way Neil looks at me that it's awful." Her eyelids fluttered. "I'm going to die."

"No, don't say that." Leah leaned forward. "You need to have hope. We get some fluids in you and get your stomach to the point where you can eat and you'll recover."

Mary reached out and grabbed Leah's arm with surprising force. "You need to make sure Neil and Aiden are all right."

"You'll pull through this."

"But if I don't, promise me you'll help them."

Leah looked down at her arm where Mary clutched it. The skin around Mary's broken fingernails turned white from the pressure. "Do you have any supplies? A stocked pantry? Any weapons?"

Mary lost her grip on Leah's arm. "No."

"Anywhere your family can go?"

She shook her head. "We're from Texas."

Leah glanced up at the wall behind Mary's bed. A vinyl decal took up most of the wall, proclaiming: *I have found the one my soul loves*. Leah thought about what Grant's death would do to her. If she made it home to find him clinging to the last moments of life, would she fall apart?

She turned back to Mary. "You're not going to die. We're going to get you the help you need."

Mary didn't say a word. She merely closed her eyes and twisted on the bed to face the closed window.

Leah watched her for a moment before leaving the room. Leaning against the hallway, she raked a hand down her face.

Staying here and trying to help a dying woman wouldn't get Leah home to her husband. It wouldn't connect her with the family she so desperately wanted to reach. But how could she walk away?

"Who are you?"

Leah looked down to see a little boy of no more than seven standing in the hallway with rumpled hair just like his father's. She smiled. "I'm Nurse Leah."

"Are you here to fix my mom?"

Leah swallowed. "I don't know if I can."

"Are you going to try?"

She stared into his sleepy little brown eyes and the

calling she'd felt since long before nursing school rose up inside. She nodded. "Yes, I'm going to try."

As the little boy trundled into his mom's bedroom, Leah walked down the hall. Neil sat on the edge of the sofa, cradling his head in his hands.

Leah cleared her throat. "I need to go to the hospital for supplies. Your wife will die without an IV."

Neil dropped his hands and stared at her with a mix of horror and desperation.

"I can't do it alone. I'll need your help."

CHAPTER FOURTEEN

LEAH

59 Parrot Lane
   North of Atlanta, Georgia
   Friday, 10:00 a.m.

"I don't see why I have to come with you." Neil Unders trudged alongside Leah as she strode toward the hospital. "You're the nurse. I spray pesticide around houses."

Leah cast a sideways glance at the man. Mid-forties. Slightly overweight. Dark circles of exhaustion and worry under his eyes.

She turned her attention back to the walk ahead. "I'll need to carry a week's worth of IV fluid and other first-aid supplies. It's too much for one person."

She didn't add in that she wanted a man along in case things went sideways. Not that Neil seemed all that capable of fighting off someone intent on destruction, but his presence couldn't hurt.

Parrot Lane sported tidy lawns and newer cars that would never run again. Tiny post-war houses and carports occupied most lots, but the people who lived on the street cared for their property more than Howie and his wife. No one stood in their driveway shouting obscenities at each other.

"How far is the hospital?"

Neil scrunched up his left eye as he thought it over. "Maybe two miles."

Leah could walk two miles in under half an hour if she tried, but Neil didn't have much go. He plodded along, one reluctant sneaker after the other. Leah glanced up at the sky. The sun still had a way to go before midday. Even at his pace, they would make it to the hospital and back before nightfall.

One more night in Tilly's company and Leah could get on with her journey. She would show Neil how to change the fluid bags and tend to Mary's IV and what to do if things went wrong. Then she would pack up and head north.

"Are you from around here?"

Leah shook herself out of her thoughts. "No. I have a house in Smyrna." When Neil lifted his brow in question, Leah filled in the gap. "I was on the way to Hampton. My sister lives there."

"How'd you get a working car?"

"It was fifty years old. No electronics."

Neil nodded, but didn't ask any more questions. They lapsed into awkward silence until Neil slowed her with a flat palm in the air. "We should cut over to the next street. Neighborhood gets a bit dicey up here."

They cut over to another street where brick ranches gave way to clapboard siding in need of paint and weedy front yards. "The area around the hospital's gone downhill the last few years. Too much noise and sirens at all hours." He snorted. "Won't be a problem anymore, I guess."

Leah nodded. She'd seen that before. No one wanted to live next door to a twenty-four-hour emergency room. "So how long have you and Mary lived here?"

Neil thought it over. "Nine years. We moved in a few years before Aiden was born."

"He seems like a good kid."

Neil brightened. "He's the best. Good-natured, listens in school, loves his mom." At the mention of Mary, Neil's voice cracked. He shoved a hand through his hair. "If we do this, will she make it?"

Leah exhaled. "I don't know. She's obviously been exposed to a significant dose of radiation. But she could recover. Lots of people in Hiroshima survived."

"Even those as sick as Mary?"

"Everything I've read said so."

Neil cut her a glance. "Are you a radiation expert?"

Leah laughed. "No. I spent the two days after the explosion trapped in a bookstore. It had a good World War II section."

A sad smile broke through Neil's grief and it changed his entire appearance. He seemed ten years younger and a million times less fragile. "Gosh, how I wish we'd known. When the power went out, we just thought it was a temporary thing, like a transformer blew or the substation failed."

"What about your car?"

"We didn't check. We both get off early on Fridays and the weekend is the only real time I have with Aiden. I didn't try to start my car until Monday morning."

"But your wife saw the blast."

"When she got home and described it—that's when I knew something serious had happened. But it was late. We didn't want to bother anyone."

"Didn't you try to make a call or check the news?"

Neil scratched at his hairline. "Everything was out of power. I didn't have a way to do it."

Leah couldn't believe it. She thought about all the time between the EMP and the nuclear detonation. Her mad rush to save the patients in the hospital; the trek out of downtown; Andy's recalcitrant neighbors. She never thought someone might be sitting at home, waiting for the power to come back on the whole time.

She opened her mouth to say something more, but Neil pointed ahead. "We're almost there."

Leah stopped. Even from where they stood, she could see the hospital was closed. No lights shone from any window. No beacon promised aid through an emergency-room door.

"What did they do with all the patients?"

Neil glanced at her in alarm. "You don't think..."

Leah swallowed. "I hope not, but I've never seen a hospital just give up before."

"Do you think we need to worry?"

"My gut says yes."

"Then let's cut over to Overton. It's a direct shot and there's a bit of a hill. We should be able to see what's happening in the parking lot a bit before we get there."

Leah nodded and followed Neil through the neighborhood and down several side streets until they came to Overton Place. He motioned for her to slow down. As they approached the top of a hill, Neil eased behind a car parked on the side of the road and Leah followed.

Creeping up the side of the car, they peered over the hood at the hospital. Leah gasped.

The hospital had been overrun. People sat in huddled masses in a clumped-up line leading away from the doors and into the parking lot. Dead cars filled almost every space. Wood covered the entryway doors to the emergency room and big neon letters proclaimed:

Hospital Over Capacity
No Power
No Aid

Neil let out an audible groan. "Are those bodies?"

Leah followed his gaze. Toward the side exit, a heap formed in the loading bay for the ambulances. An arm stuck out here and a leg there. She nodded. "Looks like it."

"Who would do such a thing?"

She'd seen it before in the history books of World

War II. When hospitals were overrun with the dead and dying, everything disintegrated into chaos. "They weren't prepared for this many sick. They must have run out of beds and supplies. When the backup generators failed..."

Leah closed her eyes and forced down a wave of nausea. "A lot of patients died."

"And then they threw them in a heap outside?"

"Many of the people who came here could have been carriers of radiation. It sticks to clothes and skin. Burning is one of the ways to ensure elimination."

Neil covered his mouth with his hand. "So that's a pyre?"

"Probably."

"We should go. There's no way we can find what we need." Neil turned away, but Leah grabbed his arm.

"We have to try. Every floor of that hospital has supplies. Your wife needs fluids. If there are any bags left inside, I can find them."

"How can we get in? Look at the parking lot!" Neil's voice rose and Leah tried to shush him. He shrugged her off. "There's people sitting out there waiting to be added to the heap. If we walk down there, we'll be mobbed!"

"I never said we'd go in the front door."

"Then how?"

Leah puffed out a breath and steeled her features. "The easiest way will be through the morgue."

Neil groaned. "I don't think I'm cut out for this."

"Do you want your wife to die?"

He stilled. "Of course not."

"Then we need to get in there and get some supplies."

"You really think she'll die without an IV?"

Leah cut the niceties. Neil needed cold, hard facts. She took his hands in hers. "Mary can't hold down a sip of water without throwing up. Her lips are cracked, her skin is like paper. If I pinch it, it stays crumpled. She hasn't gone to the bathroom in almost twenty-four hours. If she doesn't get some fluids and electrolytes in her and soon, she'll be dead in a matter of days."

Neil stared at their joined hands. "And if she does get the fluids?"

"Then she has a chance."

After a long moment, he forced his head back up. Unshed tears glassed his pupils. "Okay. Let's do it."

"Good. Follow me." Leah set off for the hospital, keeping to the edge of houses and behind stalled cars. As they closed the distance, Leah slowed, checking for any signs of movement or alert eyes before she advanced.

At last, they snaked around the main parking lot to the parking garage. Keeping to the shadows, they slinked down the levels until Leah stopped at the ground floor and a pair of sliding doors. She pointed in the gloom. "Welcome to the morgue."

"How are we going to get in?"

"We're going to walk." Without any lights, the bottom floor of the parking garage took on the quality of a tomb. No one living hung around the morgue.

With barely enough light to see, she wedged her fingers between the sliding doors. They didn't budge.

She tried again. Nothing.

"Let me try." Neil stepped forward and braced his legs a few feet apart before shoving his fingers in the gap. He grunted and pushed, but the doors refused to disengage. "It's useless."

"No. We just need a tool." Leah spun around in a circle, squinting into the corners of the garage. She walked toward the closest wall and spotted something that might work. "Here!" She rushed up to it and wrenched it out of the ground.

"What is it?"

She rushed back with a triumphant smile. "A No Smoking sign. Hospitals love to put them right by the best place to smoke." Leah wedged the metal between the doors and with Neil pulling and her pushing, the locking mechanism finally gave way.

"We're in!" Leah stepped inside and the smell of rotting flesh hit her nose. She gagged and staggered back.

Neil joined her and hacked back a cough. "What *is* that?"

Leah swallowed down her stomach. "The dead without refrigeration."

"I'm going to be sick."

"Help me shut the doors."

"What? Are you crazy? You want to trap us in here in the dark with that smell?"

Leah leaned the sign against the wall and turned to Neil. "We don't want anyone to know we're here. Come on."

CHAPTER FIFTEEN

GRANT

Boundless Sports
    Smyrna, Georgia
    Friday, 10:00 a.m.

The lock to the sporting goods store was one of those flimsy come-with-the-door types that took nothing more than a couple of jiggles and a credit card to open. Grant popped the lock and turned the knob.

"Where'd you learn to do that?"

Grant shrugged. "When you work with hackers all day, you pick up a thing or two."

The door opened with a squeak of rust against metal and Grant squinted into the dim space. The floor-to-ceiling windows out front cast enough light to make out blobs of clothing racks and shelves full of gear, but nothing determinate. Grant hesitated.

Oliver's comments stuck with him. *I'm a thief*. He

glanced back at his neighbors. He couldn't walk in that sporting goods store and walk out with a backpack full of supplies without giving something in return. But he couldn't leave empty-handed, either.

If the coming weeks were as brutal as Grant feared, he and Leah would need every last resource they could scrounge up. If he didn't take some items now, he might be reduced to worse crimes later.

"Having second thoughts?" Dan eased up beside him.

"A few."

"You can break and enter, but you can't steal?" Oliver pushed his sleeves up his arms. "Seems kind of arbitrary if you ask me."

"I haven't entered. Just broken at this point. I can lock the door and we can walk away."

"And risk getting shot like that guy lying out in the gas station parking lot? No thank you."

Grant turned to Oliver. "You're the one who called us thieves."

"And if we steal, that's exactly what we are. But I've seen the news. I know what's coming. The world will be watching us tear ourselves apart and they won't be swooping in to help."

"It's early. If we give them some time—"

Dan cut Grant off. "Then they'll come in with tanks and guns and parade us through the streets to refugee camps where we'll be branded and tagged and never be free again. No thank you. I'd rather be a thief than a refugee."

Grant pressed his knuckles to his forehead. He still needed to find his wife. If that meant searching all of downtown Atlanta for her body, he would need more than a handgun and his wits.

He shoved the doubt and shame of his choice down into the depths of his belly and motioned toward the store. "Let's spread out and clear the place first. Then we decide what comes home."

Oliver fanned out to the right, Dan took the left, and Grant took straight down the middle. After closing the door behind him, he waited, counting to one hundred as his eyes adjusted to the dark.

He pulled his handgun from the holster and held it out, ready to fire. It had been a long time since he'd gone on patrol, but his muscle memory brought it all back. *Sand. Wind. Grit always in his teeth and eyes.*

At least this time he had overpriced water bottles and coolers to contend with instead of hidden insurgents and IEDs. He cleared the middle of the store and took stock.

Occupying only a single floor, it didn't have much in the way of variety, but the sporting goods store made up for it in quality of selection. He could outfit himself for backpacking in the wild or canoeing down the Chattahoochee or paddle boarding on Lake Lanier.

All Grant cared about was surviving as everyone around him fell apart. As Oliver and Dan made their way to the front, he exhaled. They were alone.

He thought about what they would need. Apart from a case of knives, the store had no weapons. He headed straight to the backpacks. Hip packs and day packs and everything in between lined the back wall, and Grant pulled down a hunter-green hip pack that could store everything for an extended trip.

Inside went socks and water filtration straws. A mini camp stove and pellets of fuel. A compass and a Fresnel lens to start a fire with the sun. Waterproof matches and a flint fire-starter. He never wanted to be without a way to make a fire.

Next came under layers of clothes for heat and cold. Rain gear and a good two-layer jacket for himself and his wife. A solid first aid kit. It wouldn't replace the kit sitting in his car at the airport, but it would do in a pinch.

There were so many more things he needed. A fishing kit. A rifle of his own. A ton of ammo. But Grant chose to fill the rest of the pack with food. Freeze-dried meals, nutrition bars, nuts, and jerky. Everything and anything he could shove in every pouch, pocket, or crevice.

When he finished, he hoisted the pack onto his back and almost toppled to the ground. It had to weigh sixty pounds. It wasn't the most he'd carried, but it wasn't exactly light. It would be a slow walk back home.

Thought of stealing all of it made him sick, but he forced the thoughts aside. He would repay the store somehow.

He headed toward Dan across the store when a rack of watches caught his eye. He plucked off an analog number with a metal strap and put it on his wrist. Half past one. They needed to get on with it.

"Found everything you need?"

When Grant turned around the weight of the backpack almost carried him full circle.

Oliver smirked. "Guess so."

"How about you?"

The younger man held up a black messenger bag. "Five more solar panels, enough battery banks to run my gear for forty-eight hours straight, and an entire case of energy gels."

"That's it?"

The excitement dimmed in Oliver's eyes. "That's my whole list."

Dan huffed over, a massive pack as full as Grant's on his back. "How do you stand with this thing on? It's about to topple me over."

Grant waggled his pack. "Which one of these things is not like the other?"

Oliver rolled his eyes. "It's not like this place won't be here. I can always come back. Besides, you guys don't know what I've got in my pantry."

"Plenty of food, I hope."

"Enough."

Grant cocked his head.

"What? I'm a single guy and I shop at Costco."

Dan slapped Grant on the shoulder. "That's the type of place we need to hit. Get a working car and back it up to a loading bay at a Costco and fill 'er up. We could feed the entire neighborhood."

"I'll be satisfied with getting out of here and all the way home with what we've got."

"I hear you." Dan headed toward the front of the

store to check the windows.

Grant adjusted the shoulder straps of his bag and Oliver slung the messenger bag across his body.

"Fellas?"

"Yeah?"

"We might have a problem."

With his pack weighing him down, Grant trundled over to the window like a bear on two legs. "What is it?"

Dan pointed. "Look."

Grant peered between two letters on an oversized window cling and froze. A group of five men stood in the parking lot, motioning at the building and talking. From the looks of them, they weren't the security crew.

"You thinking what I'm thinking?"

Grant nodded. "Time to run out the back and hope we don't get caught."

"Exactly."

Grant hustled back to Oliver and took the man by the arm. "We need to go, now."

"What's going on?"

Grant lowered his voice as they hurried to the rear door. "Five men. Burly, tattooed. Real winners. One has a baseball bat."

Oliver shuddered. "Are they coming here?"

Dan labored to keep up. "I don't think they're looking for a puppy at the pet store."

"What if they're casing the place? Someone could already be at the back."

"It's a risk we'll have to take." Grant fingered the

Shield and cursed himself for leaving the spare magazine at home. "I've got eight rounds."

"Each rifle's good for four and I've got four more in my pocket."

Grant ground his teeth together. Could they take out five guys in a firefight? Maybe, as long as there weren't a whole pile more waiting in the back.

He motioned toward the door. "Oliver, you swing it open, I'll go first. If anyone's there, I'll shout a warning."

"What if they have a gun?"

"Then I hope like hell I shoot first."

"This can't be happening."

Dan checked his rifle. "Get used to it. This is child's play compared to what's coming."

Oliver shuddered. "Remind me next time to stay home."

"You'll be fine. We've got your back."

Oliver reached for the handle. "Ready?"

Grant nodded and the door swung open. He stepped forward into the blinding midday light.

CHAPTER SIXTEEN

LEAH

North Georgia Regional Hospital
     North of Atlanta, Georgia
     Friday, 1:00 p.m.

As the dim light from the parking garage receded, Leah's skin pricked. The stench of the abandoned morgue curdled the last of Tilly's biscuits in her stomach and she pulled her shirt up over her nose.

"I think I'm gonna be sick," Neil called out from the dark.

"We need a flashlight." Leah ran her fingers along the wall until a doorway stopped her progress. "There's usually one tucked inside most rooms for emergencies."

"Even in the morgue?"

She hesitated. "I hope so."

Clinging to the edge of the room, Leah felt in the darkness for anything that might be of use.

Light switches. A sharps container. A hand sanitizer pump on the wall.

She kept going.

Her thighs ran into a cart and something flopped against her belly. She froze. *Please don't be what I think it is.* Leah reached out with halting fingers, staggering through the darkness until her skin collided with the decaying flesh of someone long departed.

Neil called from the safety of the hallway. "Find anything?"

"Not yet." She forced down a rising tide of terror and circumvented the cart. *It's just a dead body.* She repeated it over and over in her mind, reminding herself that this apocalypse was brought on by man and not the underworld. No one was coming back to life inside the morgue.

After a series of carts, she found a storage wall. Her fingers trailed over the counter and down to handles of cabinets. One after the other, Leah opened and searched like a blind woman for something that might chase away the dark.

On the last upper cabinet, she met success. A small flashlight no bigger than her palm. She clicked it on and light flooded the room.

Leah spun around. A scream threatened to erupt from deep within her, but she willed it back with clenched teeth.

The room was filled with bodies. They lay in heaps on every cart, some two or three high. A stack of them slumped along the wall she hadn't searched, draped in hospital sheets as if they cared about their modesty.

So many dead. Leah approached the nearest gurney. A man of no more than twenty-five lay on it, burns covering one half of his face. His arm was imprinted with burns in the pattern of his shirt.

She'd seen similar photos in the books on Hiroshima: women with kimono patterns etched in black across their backs.

Another body, more burns and missing hair and sores. One after the next, each one a victim of radiation. Some so severe, they must have died within hours of arrival at the hospital.

This hospital had to be twenty miles from the center of the blast and out of the plume. If it were overrun, what must the in-town hospitals be like? Leah couldn't imagine.

"Oh, Lord." Neil stood in the doorway of the room, face as white as the sheets covering the dead.

Leah stalked up to him. "This is why your wife needs fluids. If she doesn't get them, she'll be one of these bodies. Soon."

Neil stared in detached amazement, the horror spreading across his face and numbing his features into blank incomprehension.

Leah grabbed him by the arm. "Let's get upstairs and get what we need." She tugged him along and he stumbled by her side like a member of the dying. "Get it together, Neil. I'm going to need your help."

"I didn't think... I didn't imagine..." He stopped

walking and Leah jerked as his weight whipped her backward.

"Don't think about it. Just do what we came here to do."

He ran his tongue over his lips. "We're all going to die."

"Don't be silly. You're not sick."

"No, not from radiation." He looked around him like a parched man in a desert. "We're never going to make it. Who's going to open the stores? Who's going to turn the lights back on?" He fumbled for his back pocket and pulled out a worn leather wallet.

With shaking fingers, Neil thumbed through his money. "I've got seventeen dollars. What's that going to buy me now?"

Leah let her shirt fall off her face and sucked in a breath. She'd gotten used to the smell. "We can't worry about that now. We need to focus and stay on task."

"I can't... I don't..."

"You can and you will." Leah dug her nails into Neil's upper arm and yanked him off center. "Now."

She hauled him down the hall with one hand while she held the flashlight in the other. Soon, they reached the main hub of the hospital and the useless elevators. "The emergency room will be on the first floor. We'll need to avoid it. A top floor is less likely to be ransacked."

Neil didn't say a word as Leah navigated to the stairwell. After letting him go to open the door, she practically shoved him inside. "All the way up to the top. Maybe by then you'll come to your senses."

He tramped up the stairs, one after the other, while Leah followed with the flashlight. Every time his frame obscured the beam of light, he cast ghoulish shadows on the wall ten feet high.

They reached the top of the stairwell and Leah paused to catch her breath. "Better?"

"A little."

"Good. We're looking for IV fluid, IV kits, clean needles, lines, that sort of thing."

"Probably should get some antibiotics, too."

"Your wife doesn't have an infection."

Neil pointed to Leah's head. "But you do. Those stitches look gnarly. The skin's all swollen and red."

Leah patted her scalp two inches below the wound and winced. Neil was right. If she didn't find some medicine, she might end up like all the bodies in the morgue, too. "All right. Antibiotics. But we'll probably have to find the pharmacy for those."

With a deep breath, Leah clicked off the flashlight and plunged the stairwell into darkness.

"What are you doing?"

"Taking precautions. If someone's up on this floor, I don't want to surprise them. We want to make it out of here in one piece, remember?" Leah didn't wait for Neil to argue. She pushed open the stairwell door.

Stale air wafted past her. It smelled of closed rooms and no air conditioning, but not death. She sucked in a lungful as Neil stepped into the hall beside her.

"We need a supply room. Most floors have one where

they keep essentials like fluids and syringes and high-volume supplies."

Leah set off, searching one room after the next, on and on down every hallway. From the looks of the empty rooms and orderly nursing stations, the floor had been evacuated with the power loss.

Top floors usually held offices and day rooms, not overnight patients. It made sense to close them down and concentrate on the lower floors in an emergency. If Georgia Memorial survived the blast, the administrators would have done the same thing.

She didn't know how long they searched, but it seemed like hours. At last, they found the room she needed all the way across the hospital.

Leah handed the flashlight to Neil and he held it up while she pulled together IV supplies and twelve bags of fluid. Then she moved on to instant cold packs and rolled bandages and anything else Mary could need while recovering.

When she finished, a small mountain sat on the counter.

"How are we going to carry all that?"

Leah spun around and searched the stacks of supplies. "With these." She grabbed four drawstring bags patients used for their clothes and handed two to Neil. "We can split the weight. Three fluid bags per and add the supplies on top. We'll carry two each."

Neil complied, stuffing his share into two sacks before slinging one over each shoulder. "Now you need medicine."

Leah frowned. Searching for the pharmacy didn't fill her with confidence. "I think we should skip it."

"No. You came all this way to help my wife. You need medicine and this is the best place to get it."

She opened her mouth to argue when a shout pierced the stillness. "Yo, Billy, I see a light!"

Oh, no. Leah flicked the flashlight off. "We've got to go. Now."

"We'll never find our way in the dark!"

"We don't have a choice." Leah reached out and fumbled for his arm. "Come on."

Together, they crept out of the supply room, keeping tight to the wall. Leah tried to remember the route to the stairs. They edged down a long hallway, unsure when or if they would run into the man who spotted them.

As the hall opened up to the hub in the middle of the hospital, a flashlight beam popped out of a room and landed smack on Neil's chest.

"Run!" Leah shoved Neil toward the stairwell and he took off with the plastic sacks thumping on his back.

Shouts rang out behind them and Leah urged Neil faster. He stumbled in front of her, sprawling out on the floor. Another beam of light lit up his back as he scrambled to his feet.

"They're running away!"

"Stop them!"

Neil hissed as he ran. "Who is it?"

Leah didn't want to waste time finding out. She grabbed a scrap of Neil's shirt and dragged him toward the stairs. "Just go!"

After throwing open the door, Leah rushed inside. Neil headed straight down and she eased the door shut behind her. Maybe they wouldn't follow. Maybe she would luck out.

As she hurried to follow Neil, the top door to the stairwell flew open. A flashlight beam pierced the dark. Leah flattened herself into a corner three floors down.

"See 'em?"

The beam of light tracked back and forth in slow motion. Leah squeezed her eyes shut and willed her body to disappear.

After what seemed like forever, the light retreated. "Naw, they didn't come down here."

She sagged in relief as the door shut. Five minutes later, she stumbled out the morgue entrance and found Neil in the shadows.

"Did they see you?"

"I hope not."

"Were they hospital employees?"

"I don't think so."

"Then who were they?"

Leah had no idea, but she wasn't about to go back inside and introduce herself. "If someone starts chasing you, it's a pretty good sign they aren't friendly." She wiped sweat off her forehead and bit back a show of pain. Antibiotics would have to wait. "Let's get back to your wife."

CHAPTER SEVENTEEN

GRANT

Boundless Sports
    Smyrna, Georgia
    Friday, 2:00 p.m.

Grant squinted into the sunlight, holding tight to the wall. With a stand of trees and a dumpster blocking his view, he couldn't tell if the men Dan spotted were still in the front of the store, or if any had crept toward the back.

Too late to worry about it now.

He gripped the 9mm with firm, but not tight, fingers. After years of practice and thousands of rounds, Grant had confidence in his skill. He hoped that would be enough to make any shots count.

Oliver held up a hand to block the light. "I don't see them."

Grant nodded. "Agreed."

"Let's make a run for it."

"I can't run anywhere with this pack." Dan lumbered out of the store, rifle low, but ready. "If they find us, we'll have to persuade them to leave us alone or engage."

"What do you mean, *engage*?" Oliver's voice squeaked. "We're not here to shoot anyone!"

Grant echoed Dan's comments. "Only if they shoot first."

Oliver shut the door to the store and shook his head. "This is crazy. You two are overreacting."

He stepped away from the wall and Grant hissed at him. "Get back here."

"No. You two can play cops and robbers, but I'm walking home." He pulled a pouch of electrolyte goo from his messenger bag and tore it open before sucking down the contents.

Grant watched with increasing unease. The kid was going to draw attention. He'd be spotted and then they'd all have to deal with what happened next.

He glanced at Dan. The older man shared his sentiment, scowling at Oliver as he boldly walked toward the street.

"I don't like this at all."

"Neither do I, but let's go. He's not going to make it on his own."

"Do we really need him?"

Grant flicked his eyes back to Dan. "I'm not answering that."

"Sooner or later, you'll have to make the tough choices."

"Not today." Grant stepped away from the wall and

eased through the empty loading bay. Every three steps, he scanned the horizon, sweeping left and right and back again.

As Oliver reached the street, a shout rang out. "Hey, man! Whatcha doin'?"

Grant rushed to the tree line, bobbing as the massive pack threw him off balance. He careened behind the closest trunk and landed in scrubby weeds. The weight of the pack made it impossible to move with enough speed. He unclipped the hip belt and shrugged the massive thing off his shoulders. It landed with a thud on the ground.

Without the weight, Grant crept closer to Oliver. The kid stood in the middle of the empty street, his back to Grant.

Someone outside Grant's field of view shouted again. "Whatcha got in that bag, man? Food?"

Oliver stammered. "It's nothing. Just some clothes."

"I bet it's beer. You got beer in there, dontcha? That's why you aren't interested in sharing." The voice rose as it carried farther afield. "This fella's got beer and he don't wanna share."

A chorus of boos echoed from in front of the strip mall and Grant cursed. Maybe Oliver could sweet-talk his way out of the situation.

"It's not beer. Just some runner's goo."

"What did you say? You've got some good stuff in there? We like good stuff. How about you come on over and let us take a look."

Oliver shook his head. "It's not good. It's goo. G-o-o."

He spelled out the words with a hint of frustration in his voice and Grant tensed. The kid was doing everything wrong.

Easing farther down the line of trees, Grant froze when the man came into view. Jeans. T-shirt. Strong arms and a thick neck. Grant didn't see a gun, but that didn't mean the guy didn't have one. He glanced back at Oliver. Where was his rifle? Didn't he have it?

He spun back to check on Dan. In the time Grant had been watching Oliver, Dan had made it to the grove of trees. Two rifles were propped on his shoulder as he heaved for breath. *Great*. Not only did Oliver have no sense when to keep his mouth shut, he also didn't know when to brandish a weapon.

Grant sucked in a breath. This needed to end. *Now*. He motioned to Dan to get the guns ready. The older man nodded and unbuckled his pack before sliding it to the ground. As soon as Dan brought one rifle up to his shoulder, Grant stepped out from behind the tree.

Aiming his 9mm at the man in the street, he shouted to Oliver. "Get behind me. Now."

"But—"

"Do it."

Oliver complied, easing behind Grant with his hands up.

"Find Dan. Get a damn rifle."

Oliver muttered something under his breath, but Grant didn't bother to listen. He jutted his chin at the stranger in the street. "You have an issue with my friend, you take it up with me."

The man hooked his thumbs in his belt loops. "Seems like you're the one with a problem. Way you're pointin' that gun at me and all."

Grant lifted his eyes to meet the stranger's, but didn't move his head. "We aren't interested in you or what you're doing here, so how about you leave and that'll be the end of it."

A smile spread wide and slow across the man's face, splitting his beard in two. "Now what would be the fun in that? All we want is a little conversation, ain't that right?"

Another man entered Grant's vision. Bigger than the last, with a baseball bat resting on his shoulder, he stopped beside his friend. "Have we done something to offend you?"

"He was harassing a friend of mine."

The new man raised an eyebrow. "That's an awfully big word, *harassing*. Are you sure you didn't mean making polite conversation? Because that's what it sounded like to me."

Grant inhaled through his nose and tried to calm the accelerated beating of his heart. "Just walk away and no one has to get hurt."

The new man laughed, quiet at first, then louder and louder until he had to use the bat as a cane for support. "That's a good one. Like you with that fancy little piece could ever be a match for us. I bet you don't even know how it works."

Grant knew the man purposefully pushed his buttons, but he didn't care. He needed to be put in his place. The minute Grant showed weakness, he'd be prey.

Grant refused to be prey.

He moved until the barrel of the handgun lined up with the new man's chest. "Want to find out?"

"Ooo-wee, he is a firecracker." The new guy shook his head. "Too bad there's only one of you." He turned and motioned to his right. A moment later, six guys strode out from behind the front of the strip mall. "There's eight of us."

"Still leaves me an extra bullet."

"Not if we get to you first."

As if on cue, the group charged, six burly troublemakers running full-tilt at Grant. He backpedaled with his gun in front, waiting for anyone to brandish a firearm. He didn't want to shoot first.

A crack of a shot sounded from behind him and the man closest to Grant fell to his knees. Blood bloomed across his shoulder and coated his fingers as he held them to the wound.

Grant whipped his head around. Dan stood at the edge of the trees, rifle aimed and ready. *Damn it. I didn't want to shoot anyone.*

A roar rose up from the non-wounded and Grant forced his thoughts and feelings to the back corner of his mind. This wasn't about right or wrong or how to leave peacefully anymore. It had turned into survival, plain and simple.

He wasn't going to die on a street a mile from home because he told some thug to get lost. A man with a ponytail and a Braves T-shirt neared and Grant took aim. He fired and hit the guy in the kneecap.

The man fell to the ground screaming.

"Try not to kill them!" Grant shouted at Dan as he took aim at another, clipping him in the shoulder. The man kept running. Grant cursed and fired again, hitting him this time in the thigh. He fell to the ground.

Three rounds down, six to go. He fired at the next man and hit him in the arm. He stumbled to a stop, grabbing his bicep to slow the bleeding.

Another shot rang out from the trees and Dan clipped another aggressor in the shoulder. Only three men remained: the two he'd spoken to and one more from the melee now rolling around in agony in the street. The lone man on attack slowed and looked around at his friends.

"I told you, just leave and we'll go. We don't want to hurt any of you. We just want to be left alone."

The hesitating man threw up his hands and took off, disappearing behind the building.

Grant took aim on Mr. Baseball Bat. "Just walk away."

The man tilted his head and stared at Grant for a moment. "You're tougher than I gave you credit for."

"Leave or the next bullet will be for your chest."

The man swung the baseball bat in a loose circle in front of him. "Next time we meet, we'll be better prepared."

"So will we."

Grant stood still as the two approached their

compatriots in the street, helping them limp to standing positions and hobble back toward the front of the stores.

Dan strode up, rifle still loaded and ready.

Grant kept his eyes on the retreating pack of bullies. "You didn't need to shoot."

"I can't carry two backpacks. If I hadn't shot, they'd have swarmed you."

Grant cast Dan a glance. "So you did it for the gear?"

"Of course." Dan grinned. "You think I care about saving you?"

"Where's Oliver?"

"Back behind the trees. I think he pissed his pants."

Grant exhaled and clapped Dan on the back. "Welcome to the apocalypse."

CHAPTER EIGHTEEN

LEAH

59 Parrot Lane
   North of Atlanta, Georgia
   Friday, 7:00 p.m.

Leah connected the IV to the line now running from Mary's arm and hung it on the bedpost. She smiled at the woman. "You should start feeling better in a day or two."

Neil stood beside the bed, staring at the bag of fluid. "How often do I change it?"

"For the first two days, every time it runs out. Then you can slow and gradually taper until you've used at least eight. If she's feeling better, you can stop and save the rest, but if she's not, keep going until they're gone."

Mary tried to speak, but a cough came out instead. After a few moments, she tried again. "Thank you for all you've done. I know it wasn't easy."

Leah smiled. "You're welcome."

She eased out of the room and let Neil and his wife have a few moments alone.

Aiden stood in the hallway, listening. "Is my mom going to be all right?"

"I hope so."

"What about you?"

Leah frowned. "What do you mean?"

"Will you be all right?"

"I—I—" Leah didn't know what to say. She hadn't had time to think about herself or take a break or even look in the mirror since she set off with Neil earlier that day.

Neil shut the door to the bedroom and smiled at his son. "You aren't bothering the nice nurse, are you?"

He shook his head.

"Good. Now go on and get ready for bed."

"*Da-ad.*"

"Now, Aiden."

The little boy stomped off and Neil managed an apologetic smile. "He can be a little blunt."

Leah wondered how bad she had to look for everyone to be handling her with kid gloves. She had to get out of there and back to Tilly's where she could let her guard down and assess the wound. "I should be going."

"Right." Neil stuck out his hand. "Thanks for everything. Sorry we couldn't get you antibiotics."

Leah shook it off with a nod. "It's okay. I'm sure somewhere up by my sister's place will have some." She said a few more vague pleasantries about his wife and her speedy recovery and darted out the front door.

Tilly welcomed her in with a gasp. "Lord have mercy, what did that man put you through?"

"That bad, huh?"

"You look like your head's been through a meat grinder."

Leah winced. "Can I use the bathroom?"

Tilly nodded and Leah headed into the bathroom. Clenching her teeth, she braced herself before looking in the mirror. *Oh, wow.*

Where careful stitches pulled together clean skin the day before, now there lurked a nasty, raised welt of a wound with oozing pus and swollen ridges. She reached up to her hair and let out a cry when she moved it. Her entire head burned in pain with every move of her scalp.

Leah gripped the edge of the sink and stared until the facts couldn't be ignored. *I have to open it back up. I have to drain the wound.*

She grimaced. Could she do it on her own? With no numbing agent or painkillers?

She stared at her scalp. Could she solider on and make it to Hampton without treatment? She already knew the answer. No way could she walk for miles with a festering head wound. At a minimum, it needed to be cleaned and drained.

If she didn't, she'd succumb to fever and headaches before she made it a mile down the road.

Leah leaned closer to the mirror. Maybe if she popped a few stitches it would drain and she could stave off anything worse. Leah snuffed back a wave of tears. The pain clouded her vision.

I don't have a choice.

She walked out of the bathroom and found Tilly in the kitchen already heating up boiling water on the stove. "I figure we sanitize everything as best we can. Then you douse that whole head of yours in vodka."

"What about the gin?"

"I drink gin. We aren't pouring any more of that on your head."

Leah cracked a smile. "Do you by any chance have sharp scissors and a razor?"

Tilly raised an eyebrow.

"I need to shave my head."

Half an hour later, Leah sat in front of Tilly's bedroom mirror cutting the last bit of blonde hair off her scalp. She soaped her head all over, wincing as the bubbles came into contact with her wound. Using the razor, she shaved as close as she dared to the stitches, groaning in pain as the blades ran over swollen skin.

She'd resisted doing it before to preserve her hair, but now she didn't have a choice. Every strand could collect dust and germs and bring on a worse infection. It all had to go.

By the time she finished removing the last bit of hair, the sun sank below the horizon and Tilly turned on the oil lamp.

Leah stared at her bald, angry head in the mirror. "I always wondered what I'd look like bald."

"What do you think?"

She smiled. "I look better with hair."

"Don't we all, dear." Tilly handed over a towel and the bottle of vodka. "Let's get started."

Leah draped the towel around her shoulders and clipped it tight. Tilly uncorked the vodka and held it in a shaky grip above Leah's head. "Tell me when."

Leah gritted her teeth. "Ready."

The scream that poured from Leah's mouth sounded less human than feral beast. She squeezed her hands into fists and nearly beat a hole in her thighs as the liquor coated her wound.

Tilly stopped pouring and capped the bottle. "Now comes the fun part."

Spots swam before Leah's eyes. She gripped the dresser as the room spun. "I need a minute."

Inhale. Exhale. Inhale. Exhale.

Over and over, she worked on training her breath and her heart to align. She'd seen doctors do something similar before surgery; bringing their heart and their minds to the center ensured a steady hand. Maybe it would help her.

She picked up the sharpest knife from Tilly's kitchen and held it over the open candle flame on the dresser. With the swelling of the wound, she could barely make out a single stitch. She would start with the bottom. If she were lucky, it might be enough to release the trapped infection and she could leave the rest intact.

Leah leaned closer to the mirror and searched for the invisible thread. "I should have used neon."

"All out of that, I'm afraid." Tilly patted her shoulder. "You're doing just fine."

With the knife in hand, Leah tried again. A hint of something plastic caught her eye and Leah went for it, tucking the knife between two sections of angry skin. She sawed back and forth as tears welled in her eyes. The plastic thread gave and the bottom of the wound opened.

No pus came out.

Damn it. Leah exhaled. "One more and hopefully that's enough." She repeated the process, digging for a stitch at the top of the wound. It popped free and a gush of pus followed, draining down her forehead and cheek and dripping onto the towel.

"Good heavens, that's nasty."

Leah managed a tortured laugh. "I've seen worse."

"I bet you have."

As the pus drained, Leah wiped it away with a clean washcloth. After a minute or two, it slowed and she inspected the wound. "Hit it with some more vodka will you?"

"Yes, ma'am." Tilly doused the wound in vodka again, glugging it out of the bottle while Leah bit back another scream.

When Tilly finished, Leah wiped at her face and tears. The wound was still swollen and angry, but she could see living tissue. Her skin hadn't started to die. "That should do it. If I can keep it breathing and draining, it will give me a chance."

She still needed antibiotics, but with the pus running and the tissue disinfected, she might make it to Hampton without collapsing. Leah cleaned up the mess with Tilly's help and stood up on wobbly legs. "If you don't mind, can

I sleep on your couch again tonight?"

The older woman smiled. "Of course, dear. Let's get you tucked in."

* * *

Saturday, 8:00 a.m.

Leah sat at the kitchen table with a full belly and a pounding head. Although less swollen than the night before, her wound now leaked a steady stream of fluid as it drained. She held a paper towel up to catch the dribbles.

"Are you sure you want to leave?" Tilly sat across from her, sipping tea.

Leah nodded. "I have to get to Hampton. It's been a week since the bomb. My husband has to be frantic." She thought about all the things Grant would do if he thought she were out there somewhere, hurting and unable to make it home. "I can't wait any longer."

Tilly nodded and pulled something out of her lap. "Then take this. I don't know how recent it is, but it should help." She slid a map of Georgia across the table.

Leah pushed it back. "I can't possibly. You might need it."

"And where do you think I'm going to go?" Tilly pushed the map into Leah's hand. "You need to find your husband."

"What about you?"

"I'll be fine. I've got a stocked pantry and a neighbor who owes me a pretty big favor thanks to you."

Leah smiled. "Okay." She unfolded the map and spread it out on the table.

Tilly leaned over and pointed out her street. "If you stay on Rose Garden until Medlock, it'll run right into Highway 82. That'll take you straight up to Hampton. Don't know about sidewalks, but traffic's not an issue, is it?"

Using her fingers as a guide, Leah estimated the distance to be a shade over eighteen miles. At three miles an hour and breaks on the way, she could be at Hampton by nightfall. She sighed in relief.

Only one more day.

She couldn't wait to hug her husband and sister and put the horror of the past week behind her. She stood up and gathered her things.

Tilly smiled. "You go get that man of yours and don't let anyone stop you."

"I won't." As the older woman stood up, Leah wrapped her in a fierce hug. "Thank you. For everything."

"You're welcome. Now go."

Leah took one last look around Tilly's kitchen, slung her duffel over her shoulder, and headed toward the front door. After glancing at the map, she stepped out into the early morning light.

CHAPTER NINETEEN
GRANT

Boundless Sports
     Smyrna, Georgia
     Saturday, 8:oo a.m.

After making it back to his house, Grant collapsed in a heap of spent adrenaline and exhaustion. He'd shot three people. A week without power and six days after a nuclear bomb and he'd already resorted to gunfire.

He leaned forward and rested his forearms on his thighs. There had to be a way to bring the neighborhood together. After the sporting goods store fiasco, they had to understand how serious and heavy everything was about to become.

Stan dying in the middle of the street would pale in comparison to starving kids and desperate parents. Grant thought about Stan's wife Debbie and glanced at the front door. *I should check on her. See if she needs anything.*

He stood up and the dog stood with him, keeping tight to his side. "You want to come this time?"

She looked up at him in answer and he bent to rub her head. Every time, she let him come a little closer and pet her a little more. He smiled. "All right. But it's just down the street."

Together, they walked out the front door. The dog kept close, never venturing too far from Grant despite the lack of a leash. They stopped at Debbie and Stan's front door. Grant knocked.

He glanced down at the dog. "Maybe she didn't hear me." He knocked again, this time using the side of his fist.

The door creaked open. "Debbie?"

Grant toed it wider. The dog smelled it first. She whined and ran in a circle around Grant's legs. He glanced back at the street. No one else was outside. He turned back to the house. "Debbie? Are you in there?"

The dog whined again.

"You can keep watch, but I've got to go in." Grant stepped into the house and the smell intensified. Worse than rotting garbage, it made him shield his nose and breathe through his shirtsleeve.

Grant called out again. "Debbie! Debbie where are you?"

No response.

He eased through the dark first floor, checking the empty kitchen and office, even opening the bathroom and laundry room doors. She wasn't there. Either she'd left to go visit with a neighbor or...

He hesitated at the stairs. Grant knew the smell. He knew what it meant, but he didn't want to admit it. Hadn't anyone offered to help her bury Stan? Had she lived with him all this time, decaying on her bed?

Climbing the stairs, the smell gagged him with every breath. He stopped outside the master bedroom and exhaled. "Debbie? Debbie are you in there?"

Nothing.

Grant reached for the doorknob and pushed the door open. He dropped his hand covering his mouth.

"Oh, Debbie." She lay beside her ashen husband, a plastic bag over her head. Grant remembered her words: *What am I going to do without him?*

Now she didn't have to worry. They were together again in death.

Grant pulled the door closed and descended the stairs, staring again at photo after photo of the once-happy pair who were now decomposing in their bed.

Visions of Leah crowded in his mind. Could she have suffered the same fate? He shook his head, refusing to think about his wife as anything other than alive. She had to be out there, somewhere, trying to get home. She hadn't died at the hospital. She didn't succumb to radiation sickness a day after the blast.

She was out there, and he needed to find her. Forget the prep work or the attempts to get the community to understand.

Grant needed his wife and he couldn't think about anything else until he found her.

He passed through Debbie's kitchen and froze. A set of keys with a Triumph keychain hung from a peg on the wall. Stan's vintage motorcycle.

It wasn't a Cutlass with spoke wheels, but it would navigate through stalled cars and angry mobs a heck of a lot better. Grant lifted the keys off the peg and sent up a silent prayer for Stan and his wife. He hustled to the garage and opened the door. Sure enough, Stan's motorcycle sat undisturbed, ready and waiting.

Grant hustled to the garage door and pulled it open before wheeling the motorcycle out. The dog trotted up to meet him.

"Looks like I'm taking my next trip alone."

She ducked her head.

"Sorry, girl."

Together they walked the motorcycle back to Grant's house and into the garage. He didn't think anyone spotted him.

* * *

I 0:oo a.m.

Grant hoisted himself over the seat of the motorcycle and started it up. After a sputter, it eased into a purr. He tightened the daypack on his back and pushed his sunglasses tighter against his eyes. He could do with a helmet, but the thought of wearing Stan's didn't sit right with him.

First opportunity, he would find one and claim it as his own.

He glanced back at the makeshift seat he'd fashioned out of a milk crate and bungee cords. The little dog blinked her blue eyes and almost smiled. As long as he didn't wreck or take a corner too fast, she'd be all right. She'd probably prefer a car, but a jump seat on the back of the bike would have to do.

No matter the danger, he couldn't leave her behind. The possibility of him not coming back or getting trapped somewhere haunted him, but so did the thought of leaving her alone with the back door open. Anyone could come in. She could leave.

If he couldn't find his wife, Grant couldn't bear the thought of losing the dog, too.

One of these days, he'd give her a name. Just not yet.

Grant turned his attention to the journey ahead. It had been a week since the bomb detonated in downtown and most radiation would be minimal. It would take two weeks for it to fade completely, but Grant couldn't wait any longer. Every day that passed without his wife his nerves frayed a little bit more.

Soon he wouldn't be hesitating before firing a shot. Soon he'd become a man he didn't even recognize.

His reloaded 9mm sat in its holster and the extra magazine lurked in his pack. Sixteen rounds of defense and a bike for maneuverability. It was the best he could do.

He revved the motorcycle's engine once and eased off the driveway. He hadn't ridden a bike since marrying Leah. She hated the risk. One driver who didn't look, and Grant could be a smear on the asphalt. But Leah would understand now.

If it meant he found her, he'd ride a death trap all the way to Hell.

Grant eased out of the subdivision and slowed. With a bike he could risk the highway. Even with crashes and stalled cars, he could use the shoulder. Turning toward it, he passed a solitary man ambling down the sidewalk toward the gas station.

The man stuck out his thumb, but Grant drove on. No time to help anyone today.

He gassed the bike up the on-ramp and eased through a line of empty cars. No one was waiting to smother him this time. He thought about Darlene at the rental car facility and how they'd barely made it back off the highway before stranded motorists overwhelmed them.

Had she survived the blast? Was she hunkering down with her son in her basement now that the world had changed forever?

The highway stretched for miles before him and Grant took his time, angling around cars and buses and tractor-trailers that had stopped simultaneously in the middle of rush hour. He wondered where all the owners were now. How many were dead? How many would die in the upcoming weeks?

He worked his way through the curving connector

easing into midtown. The smell of faded smoke and burnt asphalt wrinkled his nose. Even this far away, high-rises suffered from the force of the blast. Windows on the south side of every building were blown to bits.

Grant slowed as the road buckled and cracked. He couldn't go any farther on the highway. He exited and worked through clogged city streets, past shattered clumps of marble from edifices high above, and the contents of offices now exposed to wind and rain.

A woman slumped over on a bus bench, head in her hands. Grant slowed, seeking confirmation. She lifted her head. *Not Leah.*

Grant drove on.

He passed burned buildings that still smoldered. Cars flipped over on their sides, windows obliterated. Trees uprooted from the ground and tossed against high-rises like confetti. The closer he edged to downtown, the worse the destruction.

Did anyone survive here?

Grant peered into condo buildings that used to stand tall, gleaming with floor-to-ceiling windows. No windows remained. The buildings that weren't smoldering in broken, teetering heaps, stood barren like a greedy giant swept his hand through the floors and stole everything in sight.

The dog whined behind him and Grant put a hand back to comfort her.

The damage became incomprehensible. Grant likened it to a tsunami, earthquake, and volcano happening all at once. Rubble for buildings. Ash instead of parks. A car stuck three floors up in a building that used to house more law firms than could fit on the sign.

No sign of life.

No trace of Leah.

Grant knew going farther only put him at risk. He knew driving on into the heart of the blast would only confirm what he already knew. But he couldn't stop. He couldn't turn around until he stared at the crater and the horror of reality slapped him in the face.

Here and there, fires still smoldered. Grant eased around a massive pile of rubble and caught sight of an arm sticking out of the debris. He drove on.

Soon nothing recognizable remained. As midtown gave way to downtown, Atlanta turned into a war zone. No building still stood, no car sat idle. The streets were clogged with chunks of brick and stone and ash.

The road had burnt and reformed, creating rivulets of tar and paint. At the next intersection, debris blocked the entire road and forced him to turn the corner. He navigated in fits and starts, peeking down alleyways and backing up down dead ends.

At last, a road opened up before him and Grant plowed ahead. When he couldn't go any farther, he parked beside a hunk of what could have been a marble statue a week ago.

Up ahead, a gaping maw beckoned.

CHAPTER TWENTY

GRANT

Downtown
Atlanta, Georgia
Saturday, 11:00 a.m.

The crater carved out of asphalt and dirt and thousands of lives descended at least fifty feet beneath the level of the street. Grant crouched at the melted and reformed edge, staring into the void. He estimated the blast vaporized half a square mile, maybe more.

The gold dome of the capitol, obliterated. The white marble walls of courthouses and city jail, vanished. Georgia Memorial where his wife worked forty hours a week, vaporized into thin air.

He sucked in a tortured breath. Staring into the void pushed the air out of Grant's lungs. A week ago, this had been the heart of downtown, filled with people from all walks of life just trying to get by.

Tears came hot and fast, but he willed them back. His sinuses throbbed with the effort. It was one thing to stare out his bedroom window at the now-ruined Atlanta skyline and wonder. Even then he'd held out hope, thinking maybe Georgia Memorial was spared.

But no.

On some level, Grant had known it was hopeless to pretend. But he'd pushed the grim reality aside and focused on his wife and her tenacity. Despite everything, he'd believed she survived.

He reached out and ran his fingers through the broken asphalt. Was it foolish to hold onto hope?

Did Leah make it out of the hospital? Was his wife out there somewhere, still breathing? Or were her remains as invisible as the fading radiation all around him?

According to the truckers he met the night of the attack, radiation could linger up to two weeks. Crouching on the edge of the blast site a week later was a risk. Low levels of radiation still plagued the area. But Grant had to see it for himself. No more holding out false hope. No more wondering. Georgia Memorial was gone.

Now he could no longer deny the obvious: Leah died if she ignored his warnings and stayed at work.

Oh, God. Grant clenched his fists and closed his eyes. He'd give anything just to know. Did she die in the blast or make it out? Was she out there somewhere, waiting for him to save her? He didn't know how long he could go on stuck in limbo.

What if I never find her?

A soft scrap of fur rubbed across his fingers and Grant opened his eyes. *The dog.* She'd hopped out of the crate and picked her way through the debris to stand by his side.

Grant snuffed back snot and tears and premature grief. "She's not dead. I refuse to believe it." He ran his hand through the dog's fur and smiled through the pain when she didn't back away.

"We'll be okay, you and me." He scratched under her chin. "We'll be okay."

The more he said it, the more he believed it. If he repeated it enough, it might come true. He had to have faith.

At last, Grant stood. He turned to face the crumbling remains of downtown.

Leah could be out there, hurt but alive. *Suffering.* He glanced down at the dog. "You all right with staying out for a while?"

The dog looked up at him with that same patient stare that said, *I'm with you.*

Grant nodded. "Then let's look for her."

After returning to the motorcycle, Grant swung his leg over and the dog hopped back up into the crate. He started the engine and turned the bike around. Parsing downtown into sectors in his mind, he worked out his own personal search grid. Building by building, block by block, he would look for his wife.

He'd either find her or exhaust himself trying.

Grant eased down the first street, dodging debris and buckled roadway, searching for any sign of life. It was painstaking work. Traveling at speeds barely fast enough to keep the bike upright, he worked his way first east then south, turning at each passable block in a grid around the crater.

An hour into his search, something in the corner of his vision stirred. It could have been a dog or a cat or a rat rummaging through a pile of discarded rags, but Grant couldn't leave without checking it out.

He parked the bike and the dog hopped out. She sniffed the air in front of her and growled, short and low. The bundle of rags shifted against the broken concrete.

Grant glanced down at the dog. She'd reacted the same way to Stan stumbling in the street. She didn't like dying humans. "You can wait here, if you want."

The dog looked up at him, but didn't sit. As Grant took another step, so did she. He appreciated the company.

As he advanced, the smell of burnt flesh reached his nose. With his stomach roiling, Grant brought his arm up to block the noxious odor. He called out from five feet away. "Hello? Can you hear me?"

The dirty heap moaned.

Grant stepped closer.

The dog whined.

"It's okay, girl. Don't worry." Grant reached down and picked up a section of exposed rebar lying on the ground. Mangled at one end, it had come from one of the buildings nearby, ripped straight out of the concrete by the force of the blast.

Grant stuck the rounded end out in front of him.

"Hello? Do you need some help?" He nudged the top layer of fabric away with the edge of the rod.

A charred hunk of leg jerked back beneath the tatters.

Grant swallowed. He couldn't tell if it was a man or a woman. He didn't want to come any closer, but couldn't leave without being sure. What if the quivering hunk of human in front of him was his wife?

He stepped closer and the stench turned from burnt skin to stale urine and misery. Grant stifled a gag. "Please, do you need help?"

As he stuck the rebar out again, the bundle shifted, exposing more than just a leg.

Grant recoiled.

Where a man's face used to be, charred flesh and rot remained. One eyeball sat angry and exposed in an eye socket. The other was burned beyond recognition. A clump of black hair stuck up on the top of his scalp; all the rest was singed away.

A huge section of his cheek had died, leaving a hole straight through to his teeth. How the poor wretch was even alive, Grant had no idea. He stared at him, unsure what to do.

The man reached out a destroyed stump of a hand. His jaw worked back and forth, ripping his moldering cheek with every attempt at speech.

"What is it? What can I do?" Grant stepped closer.

The man's one good eye stared at him, begging.

"I can't understand you. Please." Grant could barely

stand to look at the man. Revulsion and pity warred inside him.

"K-K..." The injured man stuttered out a single letter, his one good eye darting back and forth as he struggled.

"What is it? Is that your name? Does it start with K?"

He held up his ruined arm. "K...ill."

Grant nodded. "Yes. The bomb killed millions of people."

The man pointed at his own face.

Grant's brain refused to make the connection. He shook his head. "I don't understand."

The dog whined.

"K-Kill..." The wounded man slumped back against the broken wall and thumped his chest with his stump.

Grant's eyes went wide. *He can't be asking that. Please tell me he's not...* Sticky spit clogged in the back of Grant's throat, but he forced the question out. "Are you asking me... Are you asking me to kill you?"

The man gave one tortured nod.

God. Grant covered his mouth with his hand. It was one thing to fight in the heat of battle or to defend himself against a mob dead set on causing mayhem. But kill an innocent man?

Grant stared at the stranger's ravaged face. He would die an agonizing death. Even if a hospital materialized out of vaporized dust a block away, it couldn't save him. Not with death in his tissue and burns covering his body.

That the man still lived was some kind of sick miracle. Leah had talked about patients who gave up. Severely injured, they would want nothing more than to shed their mortal burdens and take their last breaths. She couldn't do anything to ease their journey except provide a morphine drip and a comfortable bed.

Grant couldn't even do that. He pulled his gun free and ensured he had a round in the chamber. With a deep breath, he looked the man in the eye. "Are you sure?"

The man nodded again before shuddering with a final breath. His eye closed and Grant steeled himself.

It wasn't murder. He refused to see it as a crime. Even if it were, who would be there to prosecute? Only God himself. Grant wondered if he would approve.

He lifted the gun and took aim. One deep breath and a focused exhale. Grant pulled the trigger.

A single shot pierced the silence, echoing off the remains of civilization. The bullet pierced the man's skull and he slumped over, blood smearing against the broken wall behind his head.

Grant lowered the gun and turned around. The dog sat a few paces behind, waiting.

He felt the need to explain. "I didn't have a choice. I had to help him."

She watched him with inscrutable blue eyes. Did she understand? Was she judging him?

I'm losing my mind. Grant ran a hand over his face and shoved the Shield back in its holster. "Come on. We have more searching to do."

The dog hopped back up on the motorcycle and Grant cranked the engine.

* * *

Saturday, 4:oo p.m.

A handful of hours later and Grant's grip on reality hung in tatters. His eyes glassed over and he almost lost control when the motorcycle ran over a broken lump of the past.

So many dead and dying with nothing he could do. Working street by street in an ever-expanding grid, he'd managed to clear ten city blocks around the epicenter of the blast. No sign of Leah.

If she had been there when the bomb detonated, either she was crushed inside a collapsed building or already dead and never to be found. Grant glanced behind him. Even the dog had had enough.

On the fifth block, she stopped getting out of the crate, refusing to accompany him on his parade of horrors. On the eighth, she wouldn't even look at him anymore.

Grant exhaled. *It's time to go home.*

He took note of his location and turned the bike north. Tomorrow he would start where he left off. Navigating his way through downtown and into midtown, signs of life slowly emerged. A tree still standing. A living, breathing person leaning against a stalled car.

A sign for medical care.

Grant eased up on the gas. A handwritten banner made out of a sheet stretched across a courtyard to a set of low, white buildings.

First Aid Station

After pulling up to the gate, Grant stopped the bike. A handful of people in scrubs stood behind folding tables talking to ambulatory victims of the blast. A surge of hope shot through his veins. The chances of a random medical worker knowing his wife was slim, but if he didn't check...

He rubbed the dog on the head and hustled up to the makeshift waiting room.

CHAPTER TWENTY-ONE

LEAH

Highway 82
    Hampton, Georgia
    Saturday, 6:00 p.m.

Everything ached. Leah's feet began to throb around mile fifteen, her back a mile after that. The head wound still oozed fluid. Every hour Leah stopped, she checked on it with her travel mirror from her work bag, and kept going.

Thanks to the clear drainage path, the swelling in the surrounding tissue receded, but the wound still needed treatment. Without antibiotics, she risked a systemic infection. If one took hold, she could die.

Leah exhaled. According to Tilly's map, Hampton sat just beyond a bend in Highway 82. As Leah entered the long, shallow curve, she picked up the pace. It had taken all day to hike the eighteen miles.

Thankfully, everyone she'd encountered on her

journey left her alone. She didn't know if that was due to her shaved head, the gaping wound, or her look of fierce determination. It didn't matter. She'd finally made it to her destination.

As the road straightened, it transformed from a two-lane, undivided highway to a quaint main street. Squat buildings with little shops and restaurants, now dark and closed from lack of power, lined the entrance to Hampton.

Leah slowed. A pickup truck on a lift kit blocked the road, sitting parallel across both lanes. No other vehicle could enter the town.

She squinted into the fading light. No driver. No stranded motorist. *What an awkward way to stall.* Leah thought about the EMP and all the abandoned cars she'd encountered on her trek out of the city. Was Hampton just like downtown Atlanta with wrecks all over clogging the streets?

With just over five thousand people, it was a spit of a town. The chances of a perfect stall across Main Street were slim to none.

Leah approached with caution. On either side of the truck, hay bales had been stacked head-high, blocking the sidewalk. Butted tight together and lashed with rope, the makeshift walls weren't an accident.

A wave of goosebumps rose across Leah's arms.

What is going on?

Leah hiked her bag higher on her shoulder and fixed the air rifle's strap. She needed easy access in a hurry. With darkness quickly falling, Leah couldn't see past the first few businesses. Were guards standing watch? Had Hampton gone into some sort of lockdown after the bombs? If Leah could only find someone to talk to, they would let her in.

She backtracked to the nearest cross street and skirted the edge of the business district. If she couldn't get in the front, she would try the back. A block off the main section of town, houses took over. Leah had spent enough time in Hampton with her sister that she remembered the basic layout.

Quiet, residential side streets lined the main drag. They might be easier access points.

Nothing was stopping her from reaching her family.

As she navigated away from Main Street, hundred-year-old brick warehouses gave way to backyards and fences. A street sign up ahead announced another chance to enter the town.

Much like the last, a blockade prevented her access. This time, Leah knew nothing about it was accidental. She crept up to the Suburban stretching across the road. Like the truck, it wasn't occupied. Instead of hay bales, sheets of corrugated tin were riveted together into a six-foot-high impenetrable wall.

Leah crouched, peering beneath the vehicle in hopes she could shimmy her way into town. But cardboard boxes wedged between the Suburban's chassis and the asphalt prevented her attack.

She bit back a curse. *I can't get in here.*

With a forced exhale, Leah stood up and spun around, searching for any signs of life. No neighbors out for a walk. No lights in any of the closest homes. Nothing.

With the temperature dropping and the night settling in, she would lose all visibility soon. Leah wiped a sheen of sweat off her brow and squared her shoulders. *I'll make it to my sister's one way or another. There has to be an open street somewhere.*

Exhaustion and pain dampened her resolve, but Leah concentrated on her mission. No makeshift blockade would keep her out. *I will reach my family.*

Determination quickened her step and Leah hurried past dark houses and tall fences and on down the road. It would take more than a blockade to keep her out.

Built in the Roaring Twenties when railroads dominated the landscape and horses still outnumbered cars in country towns, Hampton began as an outpost for manufacturers and shippers sending their goods out of Atlanta and through the Great Smoky Mountains to the Carolinas and beyond.

As train traffic died, Hampton declined. Grand buildings lost their luster, trading in lead-glass windows for boards, and gleaming white paint for rot. But it didn't fall into obscurity as a failed ghost town.

Thanks to the crushing traffic and outsized home prices in Atlanta, Hampton's fall reversed. People who wanted no part of modern city life and urban sprawl had moved in. It was undergoing a renaissance.

Was that why they were so protective? Did they fear hordes of city dwellers would overrun the town?

Approaching the next street, Leah quickened her

step when the swoop of a sedan and the familiar shape of a light bar across the hood materialized out of the gloom. *Yes!* A police officer would help her.

She almost broke into a run. Ten feet from the cruiser, a beam of light flooded the darkness and blinded Leah. She held up her hand and stuttered to a stop.

"Identify yourself." The man's voice, firm with authority, sent a shiver down Leah's spine.

She dropped her hand and squinted into the light. "Leah Walton."

"Resident?"

"No."

"Then you need to turn around and leave." The cop kept the flashlight trained on Leah's face.

"My sister lives here. Dawn Minter."

"Got any proof?"

Leah glanced at the duffel on her shoulder. She had identification, but it wouldn't share the same last name. She looked up, hope in her voice. "We look exactly alike. Dawn's maybe an inch or two taller, but we have the same hair and eyes. You have to know her."

The flashlight beam bobbed. "Don't know any skinheads in Hampton."

Leah frowned. *Skinheads?* She reached up and ran her hand over her shaved stubble and groaned. Hairless and sporting a gnarly wound, she probably looked like a drug addict hoping for a score.

She tried again. "I was in a car accident trying to get here. I had to shave my head to put in the stitches."

"If you're injured, you should turn around and head back to town. We don't have a hospital here."

Leah clasped her hands in front of her. "Please, you have to know my sister. She lives on Iris Street with her husband, Chris. They've lived here almost five years. I think Chris even volunteers with the police force."

"If you don't have ID, you need to leave."

Leah's voiced edged into panic. "You don't understand. I have to get in. My husband should be there with my sister, waiting for me."

"Husband's name?"

"Grant Walton."

"Resident?"

Leah's shoulders fell. "No."

"Then it seems you're out of options, ma'am. I'm going to tell you one more time. You need to leave. Now."

Leah chewed on the inside of her cheek. *I can't leave. I've come all this way.* Grant was a mile down the road, inside her sister's house, frantic with worry. She had to get to him.

Leah took a step toward the light.

"Stop right where you are."

"I have to get in there. If you'll just make some calls, someone knows my sister."

"Rules are rules, ma'am."

Leah took another step.

"Ma'am, if you take another step, I will have no choice."

"No choice but to do what?"

The flashlight beam bobbled. "My orders are to shoot anyone who tries to come in."

"Shoot me?" Leah's voice rose in disbelief. "Don't be ridiculous. I told you Dawn lives here. What do you think she's going to do when she finds out you shot her only family?"

Frustration stole Leah's intellect. She couldn't think of a way to convince the cop to let her pass. It had only been a week since the bomb. Had things gotten so bad all the way out here that a little town like Hampton had to shut its doors and not let anyone in?

Leah pressed a palm to her forehead, using the pain of her wound to bring her clarity. Between the barricades and the cop, she wouldn't be getting inside Hampton easily tonight. She took a step back. Could she sneak in through someone's yard? Climb over one of the barricades?

What if a cop were waiting in the dark on every street? She couldn't risk getting shot just to cross the town line. Leah spun around and stared out. Thanks to the cop's flashlight, she could see twenty feet or so down the road. A wood sign on the corner proclaimed, "Welcome to Hampton, Georgia. Population 4,993."

Leah set her jaw and walked straight toward it. She turned back to face the police cruiser and the light and sat with legs crisscrossed on the sidewalk, three feet past the sign.

After a minute, the flashlight beam wavered. The cop's voice rang out. "Ma'am. I asked you to leave."

"I did."

"I can still see you."

"Am I inside the town limits?"

The flashlight beam lowered, tracking the road. The cop's voice came back neutral and cold. "No."

"Then I've complied with your request."

"What are you are going to do?"

"Sit here until you either let me in, or daylight comes and I can talk to someone else."

The flashlight clicked off and plunged Leah into the now-full darkness of the night. A radio crackled. "This is Officer Kelly. I have a situation on Begonia."

Leah exhaled in relief.

CHAPTER TWENTY-TWO

LEAH

Corner of Begonia and Lake
  Hampton, Georgia
  Saturday, 8:00 p.m.

Leah blinked as her eyelids turned red from a source of light. At some point, she'd slumped over and let exhaustion steal her consciousness. It had been a rough few days.

She ran a hand over her cheeks and opened her eyes.

Muffled voices carried from the direction of the police cruiser. Leah strained to listen, but she couldn't make out the words.

A chill shook her limbs and Leah stretched her stiff legs, now cold from the concrete, out in front of her. Whoever was out there, presumably arguing about her, needed to get on with it or turn out the light. If they weren't going to let her in, she'd rather sleep on the side of the road.

At least with a cop standing guard she didn't have to worry about her safety even if she was being treated like a criminal.

The flashlight lowered and Leah blinked back the spots swimming in her vision. A circle of light bobbed and weaved around the police car and down the sidewalk. It stopped at Leah's outstretched feet.

A pair of men's legs covered in jeans and work boots stood in front of her. She squinted as she looked up, unable to discern the man's features thanks to the light.

"Leah?"

A familiar voice filled her with hope. "Chris?"

The figure bent into a crouch and her brother-in-law's face came into view. "Is that really you?"

She smiled. "I knew if someone called you they'd figure out this was a big misunderstanding."

"You look like hell."

Leah fingered her scalp. "Car accident. I haven't been able to reach a hospital."

He pressed his lips together. "Are you sick?"

"No. Just the head wound."

After a moment, he nodded. "All right. Come with me."

"Where are we going?"

"Home." Chris held out his hand and Leah accepted it with gratitude. She would finally be able to hug her family.

"Did you wake Grant? Does he know I'm here?"

Before Chris could respond, the police officer came forward. "She's a real troublemaker, this one."

"She's my wife's sister. Seems to run in the family."

The cop snorted out a laugh. "Give Dawn my respects."

"Will do, Jim. Thanks." Chris led Leah through the narrow gap between the police car and the closest fence and into Hampton.

The silence engulfed them. Apart from their shoes slapping against the pavement, only the occasional owl or cricket cut through the dark. Chris headed straight down Begonia Way and Leah followed a step behind.

She had a million questions, but the night air stilled her tongue. She could wait until they reached the relative comfort of the house. It had taken a week to get there. A few more minutes wouldn't hurt.

While Chris led the way with his flashlight and determined steps, Leah glanced around. Not a single candle burned in any window. The stars pricked the sky above her, but apart from their scattered glow and Chris's flashlight, the town sat dark and ominous.

She adjusted her bag on her shoulder as Chris turned onto Iris Street. Four houses in, he beckoned Leah up the driveway. She hustled, almost running to pass him up the steps. Tugging the door open, Leah rushed into her sister's little bungalow.

Dawn sat at her worn wood kitchen table, a candle casting shadows across her face. As she stood up, Leah rushed into her arms. "You're safe!"

Dawn smiled against her cheek. "We are." She pulled

back and her face slipped into a frown. "But you look like an extra from *Fight Club*. What the heck happened?"

Leah winced. "Car crash. It looks worse than it is."

"I sure hope so."

Leah rose up on her tiptoes to peer down the hall. "Did you let him sleep?"

"Who?"

Leah's brow tucked. "Grant, of course."

Her sister's eyes flicked up to find her husband. "You didn't tell her?"

Chris hesitated. "I thought you should."

Dawn drew back with a frown. "Of course. Leave the hard part to me."

"She's your sister."

Leah turned to Chris. "What's going on? Where's my husband?"

Her sister squeezed her arm and dread whooshed through Leah's veins.

"He's..."

Leah twisted back to face Dawn. "He's what?"

"Not here."

All of Leah's hopes and prayers and wishes shrank to a tiny pinpoint of white-hot light and imploded within her. A swirling black void took their place. "He told me to meet him here. That this is where he was headed."

She struggled to stay standing.

Dawn gripped her arm tighter. "You should sit down."

Leah sagged into a kitchen chair. Had Grant died trying to make it home? Did he get trapped in Charlotte and suffer the same fate as so many of her friends and coworkers in Atlanta?

A sob rose up her throat, but Leah forced it down. Crying wouldn't solve anything. Not now. She glanced up at her sister.

With a scrubbed, makeup-free face, and her hair pulled back in a ponytail, Dawn could have passed for eighteen. A million memories rushed through Leah's mind.

Surviving first the death of their father when Leah was only seventeen and Dawn fifteen. Enduring the death of their mother a year later. College, then marriage, then the prospect of babies.

Through it all, Leah had supported her sister and vice versa. But somewhere along the way, Grant had become her rock. Grant had become the sure thing. Not just Leah's shoulder to cry on, but her sounding board, her solid footing, her everything.

Without him...

Dawn slid into the chair across from Leah and reached for her hand. "Tell me where you've been. What's it like out there?"

Leah blinked back her fears and worry. "When the EMP hit, I stayed past my shift, helping triage at the hospital as best I could. But after listening to Grant's voicemails..."

Dawn squeezed her hand.

"I left with an ER doctor first thing last Saturday morning. The streets were chaos. Stalled cars everywhere. We found an old station wagon that still ran and drove to Andy's house on the north side of town. I dropped him off and aimed to come straight here."

"Then what?"

Leah focused on her sister's unblemished face. "The nuclear bomb happened. I barely made it into a bookstore before the radiation began to fall."

Her sister swallowed.

"After I ran out of food and water, I risked leaving." Leah thought about the men in the Walmart and Neil Unders and his wife. "Anyone exposed to the radiation plume is sick at this point. Maybe even dead."

Her sister pulled back her hand. "How many people?"

Leah frowned. "Millions in Atlanta. I can't imagine how many more all across the country."

Chris spoke up for the first time. "How do you know that?"

Leah turned on him, shock in her voice. "I saw the blast with my own eyes. I treated people sick with radiation poisoning." She swallowed. "I waded through hundreds of dead bodies covered in burns to get medical supplies."

Dawn recoiled. "All here, in Georgia?"

"Yes. Here." Leah shook her head at her sister and brother-in-law. "Why are you acting like this is news?"

Chris crossed his arms. "Our sheriff hasn't gotten official confirmation of any bombs. So far, we only know for sure about the power outage."

Leah stared at her brother-in-law like he'd just confessed to growing up on Mars. "You won't get confirmation. All the officials are dead. They were probably vaporized into thin air the second the bomb went off."

"Seems like a pretty convenient explanation to me."

Leah couldn't believe what she was hearing. Conspiracy theories abounded on the internet, everything from the assassination of JFK to 9/11 to the president secretly being a plant from Russia. But she never thought her own family would doubt the truth.

She blinked and tried to keep the shock from her voice. "You're seriously standing there telling me you don't think the country was attacked? That nuclear bombs didn't go off all over the United States and throw us into chaos?"

Her sister tugged on her hand. "There's something we need to tell you."

Leah spun around. Dawn's lower lip quivered.

"What is it?" Leah leaned in, a million horrors running through her mind. "Is something wrong? Are you sick? Were you exposed?"

"No. It's not about me. It's...about Grant."

Leah held her breath.

"He was here."

"He's alive?"

Dawn nodded. "He came here, looking for you."

The promise of a future filled Leah with hope. She rushed out her questions without thinking. "Where is he? Is he out collecting supplies or working with law enforcement? When will he be back?" She couldn't wait to wrap her arms around him.

Her sister faltered and pulled her hand away. "Chris... We... sent him away."

Leah jerked back. "What?"

"Chris didn't...I didn't—"

"He was acting crazy." Chris ran a hand through his hair and focused on the wall above Leah's head. "He showed up here in a hot-wired car, ranting about the end of the world and a supposed nuclear holocaust."

"But it's true. All of it."

Chris crossed his arms. "We don't know that. Not for sure."

"He was erratic and talking crazy." Dawn managed a pained smile. "We thought maybe he was on drugs."

Leah tilted her head and stared at her sister. "You thought Grant was on drugs? *My* husband?"

Dawn pressed her fingertips to the wood table and her voice shrank to barely above a whisper. "I've seen it before. The ranting about things that aren't true. The stealing. It was the logical conclusion."

Leah swallowed. Comparing Grant to Chris before he got sober wasn't fair. She shook her head. "You know him. You know he's never taken drugs."

"We made the best decision under the circumstances."

Leah turned on her brother-in-law. "The best decision? You kicked my husband out after the worst terrorist attack in history because you refused to believe him and now you have the nerve to tell me it was the best decision?"

She stood on shaky legs, barely able to contain her

fury. "He told me to meet him here. I risked *everything* to get here. My life. My sanity. Everything. And you sent him away!"

"We're sorry, Leah." Dawn reached for her again, but Leah jerked her arm away.

"All this time, the only thing that kept me going was the hope of finding Grant. That he would be here, waiting for me." She focused on her sister. "How could you do this?"

Dawn forced out the words. "We were afraid."

Leah closed her eyes. Her husband was out there, somewhere. *Alive.* If it weren't for Dawn and her husband, they would be together. Leah sucked in a breath and tried to focus.

This wasn't the end of the world. She could survive this.

She opened her eyes and asked the only question left. "Where did he go?"

Her sister eased back down into her chair. "I'm sorry, Leah. But I don't have any idea."

CHAPTER TWENTY-THREE

GRANT

Downtown
   Atlanta, Georgia
   Saturday, 8:oo p.m.

"Can you hand me that bag of fluid?"

Grant reached behind him and grabbed a clear bag that nurses hook up to IVs and held it up. "This one?"

"Yep. Thanks."

He smiled at the nurse as she took it and hooked it up to a rolling IV cart. Over the course of the day, his outlook on life had swung from hope, to the depths of despair, and back to hope again. The second he walked into the waiting area, able bodied and lucid, the nurses put him to work.

During the past four hours, he'd fetched supplies, held down patients while they thrashed about, cleaned up noxious messes, and otherwise worked his backside off. He'd even rigged up flashlights to a hanging rack for makeshift nighttime lights.

Grant hadn't been filled with this much purpose since the bombs went off.

Even the dog had gotten into the act, weaving through patients and allowing them to pet her and cheer themselves up. Gone was the shy little thing that couldn't stand to be touched, and in her place, a courageous animal that wanted to help.

Grant washed his hands for the twentieth time in the portable scrubbing station set up in the rear of the clinic. While helping banished the gloom from his mind temporarily, it didn't get him any closer to finding his wife. He'd asked all the nurses, but so far, no luck. They didn't know Leah, and no one had seen a blonde nurse matching her description.

He needed to head home.

As Grant whistled for the dog, a healthy man strode into the clinic, white doctor coat a stark contrast to the dirt and grime all around. He lifted a hand to catch a nurse's attention. "I'm an ER doctor from Georgia Memorial. What can I do to help?"

Before a nurse could whisk the man away, Grant closed the distance between them. "Did you say Georgia Memorial?"

The doctor frowned in Grant's direction. "Yes, I did." Tall, with brown hair and gaunt cheeks, he didn't look familiar. But Grant didn't know many of Leah's coworkers.

"Do you know Leah Walton?"

"Who are you?"

"Her husband, Grant."

The doctor gave him the once-over, inspecting everything from his stubbled chin to his dirty boots. "I hope you don't mind, but do you have any ID? It's been a crazy few days."

Grant fished his wallet from his back pocket and flipped it open. On one side sat his driver's license, on the other, a photo of Leah on their honeymoon.

The doctor's shoulders sagged. "Didn't she make it to her sister's place?"

"So, you know her?"

"She saved my life." The doctor held out his hand. "Andy Phillips."

Grant shook his hand and pressed on. "She survived the blast?"

Dr. Phillips nodded. "Thanks to her, so did I. She's amazing, that wife of yours."

A pang of jealousy shot through Grant, but he kept his voice even. "When's the last time you saw her?"

The doctor drummed his fingers across his forehead, thinking. "A few hours before the blast. She drove me to my neighborhood and tried to convince everyone to get into the clubhouse basement."

"Did it work?"

Dr. Phillips paused. "Trying to convince a bunch of middle-class families that we're about to be bombed back into the stone age isn't exactly easy."

Grant snorted. "Sounds familiar."

"But Leah did the best job she could. Thanks to her, about half the neighborhood survived the worst of it."

"And the rest?"

Dr. Phillips pressed his fingers to his lips. "The last one died this afternoon. That's why I'm here. I figured there had to be somewhere I could help."

"And we need it." A plump nurse with a raised eyebrow stood a step away, fists on her hips. "If you two are done gabbing, we need some help."

Grant held up a hand. "Just one more minute."

She rolled her eyes and muttered something under her breath.

Dr. Phillips smiled. "I'll be there in a moment."

The nurse walked off in a huff.

"Do you know where Leah was headed?"

Dr. Phillips nodded. "Exactly where you told her. To her sister's place."

Grant blinked in slow motion. "I checked, and she wasn't there."

The doctor shrugged. "I'm sorry. That's all I know. She dropped me off at my house and headed north." He explained to Grant where he lived and what roads Leah might have taken toward Hampton.

Grant thought it over. "Do you think she could have made it out of the radiation area before the blast?"

"I don't know. We crawled through the city streets, but the roads might have opened up to the north."

"If she didn't make it to safety..."

Grant left the rest unsaid, but the doctor finished it.

"Then she's probably dead."

Grant nodded. "Thanks for your time."

"Good luck. I hope you find her. If you do, tell her thank you." He paused with a strange sort of smile. "And that I've quit smoking for good."

As he headed out of the makeshift clinic, Grant called the dog to his side. He didn't know if Leah survived the exposure to radiation, but thanks to Dr. Phillips, his search had changed. No more scouring the wreckage of the blast site. He needed to set his sights farther north.

He checked the analog watch on his wrist. *After nine already.* Searching now would be pointless. His best option was to head home, get a good night's sleep, and start fresh in the morning. Leah was out there somewhere and he wouldn't quit until he found her.

CHAPTER TWENTY-FOUR

LEAH

83 Iris Street
   Hampton, Georgia
   Saturday, 10:00 p.m.

Leah could barely process the words out of her sister's mouth. First, she kicked Grant out of her house for speaking the truth, then she didn't bother to find out where he was going.

They might look the same, with prominent cheekbones and blue eyes that shifted from cornflower to aquamarine depending on the day. They might have shared the same bedroom when they were kids.

But that was all. She couldn't be more unlike her sister if she tried. She glanced at Chris, half-asleep on the couch. Most of the reasons why were too busy sulking in the living room to be of any use.

Leah swallowed down a wave of regret and pain and

stood up. She'd sat at the kitchen table for an hour while her sister tried to explain their rationale and the town's reluctance to admit the truth. All Leah heard were excuses and fear. Hampton didn't have the answers.

She reached for her bag and air rifle and hoisted them over her shoulder.

"What are you doing?" Her sister pushed back her chair with a screech.

"Leaving."

"To where?"

"Home. It's the only place left. If Grant isn't here, then he's got to be there."

Dawn glanced at the living room. "It's not that simple."

"What do you mean?"

"You saw the roadblocks."

Leah waved her off. "I can get out the same way I got in. I'm sure that officer would love to see me leave."

Dawn's voice grew more insistent. "You don't understand."

Leah huffed out a breath. "Then explain it to me."

"After Grant left, things around here changed. The sheriff gathered everyone together and explained how they couldn't reach anyone at the power company. That no one was talking on official channels about what happened or what it meant. Rumors were flying."

"You said all this already as part of your excuse for not believing him."

Dawn ignored the slight and carried on. "Some people claimed it was war. That we were invaded on the coast and it was only a matter of time before they reached us here."

"That's crazy."

"Any crazier than a bunch of nuclear bombs all going off at once?"

Leah frowned. "But we know that's the truth."

"Do we? None of us saw the blast downtown. Grant was the first person to mention anything about bombs. We just thought it was a power outage. Something wrong with the local power plant, that was all."

"Here we go again." Leah crossed her arms. "You should have listened to him."

"All it would have done is make things worse." Chris clambered up off the couch and wiped sleep from his eyes. "The town would have gone into full militia mode instead of just lockdown."

Leah shook her head. "What do you mean, lockdown?"

He scrubbed his face. "Just what it sounds like. The town is closed. No one in. No one out."

"I got in."

"Not without almost getting shot." Dawn smoothed back her hair. "Chris went out on a limb to get you in here. You can't just change your mind."

"That's ridiculous." Leah couldn't believe the words coming out of her sister's mouth. Admitting to shoving Grant out the door because he spoke the truth was one thing, but now claiming Leah couldn't leave? She understood caring about the safety of the town, but this sounded more like a prison. "They can't keep people from leaving."

Chris's jaw ticked. "You're only here because you're family, Leah. Now that the border's closed, that's it. They'll detain you if you try to escape."

Leah palmed the back of her head. "You're serious? This isn't some made-up story just to get me to stay?"

"It's true."

Dawn didn't look like a liar.

Leah spun around in a circle, panic rising in her throat. She risked her life to get to Hampton and now that she wanted to leave, they wouldn't let her. "What happens if I try?"

"Probably the same thing that would have happened before."

"I'll get shot?"

"That or arrested and thrown in jail."

"I can't stay here. I need to find Grant."

Dawn threw her a bone. "He might come back."

Leah turned on her. "No one will let him in!"

She winced. "Maybe we could get him in, too."

"No. No way. I can't stay here. I have to find Grant." Leah looked all around, canvassing her sister's house. She couldn't just walk out the way she came in. She needed a plan. "Do you still have all that camping gear?"

Leah strode to her sister's hall closet, oblivious to anything but her newfound mission. "I need a backpack. Something better than this duffel."

"Slow down." Dawn stood up. "Weren't you listening? You can't leave."

Leah ignored her and opened the door to the closet. Clear tubs were stacked on the floor and Leah dragged them out into the dim candlelight.

"Put all that away and come back to the table. We can talk this through."

"No. I need to get out of here. Where's that daypack you used when we hiked Lookout Mountain?"

"I think I gave it to Goodwill."

Leah popped the lid on the first tub and tossed it on the floor. She rummaged through the contents and pulled out a forest-green bag. "Did not. It's right here."

With the backpack in one hand and the duffel in the other, Leah hurried back to the kitchen table. She dumped the inside of her bag across the wood and began to sort the contents.

"Leah, you need to take a step back and think about this. The police have strict orders."

She focused on her things, putting nonessentials like her ruined shirt and torn-up scrubs in one pile and her remaining two bottles of water and handful of power bars in the other. "I'll need more food and water to make it all the way home."

Leah tallied up how much she would need before digging out her wallet. She was down to her last few dollars. "Any chance you can spot me some cash? There's got to be somewhere along the way that still has food. I'll need to find some in the morning."

Dawn reached out and grabbed her arm. "Leah, stop."

She shoved her sister off. "No. I have to find Grant."

She added her flashlight and other supplies to the backpack and zipped it up.

Chris stomped up to the table. "That's enough! You have to sit the hell down and knock this off." He yanked out an empty kitchen chair and pointed at it.

Leah scoffed. "Are you going to make me?"

His lips thinned. "If I have to."

She picked up the air rifle. "Try and stop me."

"Leah! Chris! Guys, come on." Dawn tried to interject, but it was useless.

Chris gripped the back of the chair so hard his knuckles turned white. "Stay out of this, Dawn."

"Yeah, why don't you do that, just like you stayed out of the decision to kick my husband out."

"I did not!"

"Right. Like it was your idea." She jutted her chin at Chris. "You're the arbiter of all things now, aren't you? The one who gets to decide if people are crazy or telling the truth. The one who picks who stays and who goes."

Leah walked up to Chris and poked him square in the chest, twisting her index finger until she left a nail mark in his shirt. "It's your fault Grant isn't here."

Chris looked down at her finger, but he didn't remove it. "We haven't seen anything to prove a bomb went off."

Leah dropped her hand and rolled her eyes. "You're still going to pull that card? You seriously expect me to believe no one out here saw the giant ball of light or noticed people dying from radiation all over the city?"

"We thought Grant was on drugs."

"And you're the best judge of that, right?" Leah shook

her head. "A former alcoholic who sees addicts in everyone he meets."

"Leah."

She spun on her sister. "Don't you 'Leah' me. I'm right and you know it." Leah saw the hurt in her sister's face, but she couldn't stop herself. All the pent-up rage and frustration at the situation came pouring out of her mouth. "All these years, I bit my tongue and went along while you married a fixer-upper. But look how it's turned out."

"You don't mean that."

She grabbed the backpack and hoisted it on her back. "I never should have come here."

"Leah, please. You're going to get hurt."

"Been there, done that." Leah strode toward the door, ignoring her sister's pleading.

Chris beat her to the door. He stepped in front, blocking her way. "Grant was acting crazy. Bloodshot eyes, all strung out. Stolen car. He wasn't right in the head."

Leah glared at her brother-in-law. "Let me go."

"You should stay. For Dawn."

"I have to find my husband."

They stood in silence, staring each other down, neither one willing to concede.

"Chris, let her go." Dawn walked up to the pair, a twenty-dollar bill in her hand. She held it out to Leah. "It's all I have."

Leah sucked in a breath and took the money. "Thank you."

"Be careful out there."

"I'm sorry I yelled at you and—"

Dawn held up a hand. "I understand. You need to find Grant."

Leah nodded, a rush of conflicting emotions waging war inside her heart. Her sister was wrong, but Leah still loved her. "Take care of yourself." She wrapped Dawn up in a quick hug before pulling away.

Chris still stood in front of the door. "This isn't a good idea. She's putting our safety at risk by leaving."

"It'll be okay." Dawn nodded at her husband. "Let her go."

He frowned at Leah. "Don't come back."

She barely kept the scorn out of her voice. "Don't worry, I won't."

Chris opened the front door and Leah stepped out into the dark.

CHAPTER TWENTY-FIVE

LEAH

83 Iris Street
   Hampton, Georgia
   Saturday, 10:00 p.m.

Crouched at the edge of her sister's house, Leah waited for her eyes to adjust to the dark and her mind to stop spinning. Never in a million years did she expect things to devolve the way they did inside. How could her sister and brother-in-law be so shortsighted? How could they kick Grant out instead of taking him at his word?

She frowned at the cloudless sky. If Hampton closed itself off from the rest of the country, would she ever see Dawn again? The thought of losing her sister gnawed at her insides, but Leah had no choice. Her husband mattered more.

Leaving Grant alone out there to face the future without her wasn't an option. Wherever he was, she would find him. Leah sucked in a breath. Hiking to Smyrna would be difficult at best. She would need to conserve her strength.

Adrenaline carried her through the argument with Chris and her sister, but as it faded, her whole body trembled. Leah reached up and prodded the wound on her scalp. Less swollen than before, but the lack of draining fluid concerned her.

Was a latent infection building back up inside the wound? Would she succumb to its effects before she made it home?

Leah glanced back at her sister's dark house. *I should have asked about pain meds or antibiotics.* The shock of it all clouded her judgment and turned Leah reckless. She said things she didn't mean and hurt her sister out of anger.

Could she go back? She shook her head. Chris would never let her leave a second time without a massive fight. She couldn't do that to Dawn.

With a deep breath, Leah stood up. Thanks to a three-quarter moon, she could make out enough to see. It was time to leave Hampton behind.

As she walked down the driveway, the door to the house opened. Leah didn't look back.

"Leah! Wait!" Her sister hissed into the dark.

Leah stopped, but didn't turn around. "I'm not changing my mind."

"I don't want you to. I know you need to find Grant." Dawn hurried up to her side. "But you'll never get out without my help."

"What about Chris?"

Dawn glanced at the house. "He doesn't know I'm out here. He fell asleep on the couch."

"Already?"

"It's been a long day."

Leah took her sister by the arms. "I'm sorry, Dawn. I shouldn't have yelled at you and said all those things."

"It's okay. You're right, we never should have kicked Grant out. I knew it was wrong, but I was scared and... I let Chris take charge. I'm sorry."

Leah hugged Dawn again. "It's okay. I understand."

"Do you have a plan?"

"Not yet. I was hoping I could find a way to sneak through a fence or a backyard."

"It'll take you forever to get home without a car."

Leah glanced at her sister's vehicle. "Yours can't possibly work."

Dawn held up a key. "No, but my father-in-law's pickup still runs."

"What are you saying?"

"Take it."

"Doesn't he need it?"

"With the town on lockdown and nowhere to go? Hardly. The only reason it still runs is because Chris drives it around the block a few times a month. John hasn't driven in years."

"I don't know. Won't Chris be mad?"

"Madder than a box of frogs, but I can handle him."

Leah hesitated. "How am I going to get out with a

pickup truck? It's not like the cop will just wave me on through."

"There's a farm on the north edge of town. It's got a fence, but that's all. If you get going fast enough, you can bust right through it and onto the road out."

"All the way across town? There's no way. Someone will spot me."

"I'll help."

"How?"

Dawn smiled. "You leave that to me." She shoved the key in Leah's palm. "Just drive."

Thirty minutes later, the sisters sat side-by-side in a beat-up old truck with a frayed and stained bench seat and a window stuck a quarter of the way down. "You really think this'll work?"

"Yep." Dawn seemed almost giddy with excitement. "Just let me out south of the farm. Once you see a bunch of lights, gun it for the fence line."

Leah exhaled. "What happens if you get caught?"

"You'll have to drive faster, I guess."

Gripping the steering wheel with both hands, Leah bounced and bobbled through the side streets of town, navigating without headlights under her sister's directions. With the speedometer hovering around five miles an hour, she hoped the near-idle of the engine didn't penetrate through eighty-year-old siding and single-pane windows.

"Will they chase me once I'm outside city limits?"

Dawn scrunched up her face in thought. "Doubt it. If this works, they'll be too busy."

Leah nodded and focused on the road. In a matter of minutes, her sister pointed out the farm.

"It starts here. Let me out on the side and ease down the gravel until you see the first fence. Wait for the lights."

Dawn reached for the door handle, but Leah grabbed her arm. "I love you."

Her sister smiled. "I love you, too." Without another word, she hopped out of the truck and disappeared from sight.

Leah turned the truck off the asphalt and onto the rutted gravel drive. Slowing to almost walking speed, she hoped the dark hid the trail of dust kicked up in her wake. After an agonizing few minutes, a white post and rail fence came into view. She rumbled to a stop.

All she could do now was wait.

Leah turned around in the driver's seat and stared out at the little town of Hampton. Idyllic setting. Quiet nights. Crazy rules.

She didn't want any part of it. Too bad her sister didn't agree. Maybe after things calmed down and the country began to rebuild…

But Leah didn't know how long that would take. Was the president still alive? What about the rest of the government? How could anyone govern without electricity today?

She thought about the news report from Los Angeles. If parts of the West Coast still had power, would the government relocate there? Would the country end up with a version of the White House in Colorado or Wyoming?

What if there were no one left to lead? What if the perpetrators of the attack intended to invade? Would everyone become slaves to some foreign power?

Leah pressed her fingers to her temples to slow her runaway thoughts. She couldn't go down this road, not when she hadn't even escaped Hampton.

As she stared out into the dark, the first inkling of her sister's plan filtered through the open window. *Is that...?* Leah leaned over and cranked the passenger side window down. She leaned back with a laugh. *Pigs.* Her sister had let loose the farm's pigs.

Oinks and grunts sounded from the front pasture, followed by neighs and moos and a million other barnyard noises. *Is that a duck?*

Leah couldn't tell the animals apart once they all got in on the action, braying and hollering and causing a ruckus. Orbs of light followed, bouncing around the front of the property while more came from the road. That was her cue.

Leah put the truck in drive and punched the gas. The fence rose up fast in the windshield, but Leah braced herself. The wood splintered like a shot and Leah kept going, pushing the accelerator down as hard as she could while still keeping a grip on the wheel.

Rows of crops slowed her down and the truck slipped sideways on a patch of mud. *Come on.* She squeezed the steering wheel tight and sat tall on the seat, angling for the second fence line a hundred yards on.

Noises increased behind her, but Leah didn't dare turn around. If they were following her, she'd just have to outrun them. With a final punch of the accelerator, she broke through the second fence and bounced onto the road. The front fender of the truck scraped the asphalt and Leah rose off the seat.

As the truck bottomed out, she landed hard and bounced, hitting her knee on the steering column. But she made it. The little state road opened up in front of her and in half a mile, Leah turned west toward home. Daring the truck up to highway speeds, she didn't slow down until the town of Hampton was no more than a bad memory.

She hoped her sister escaped the wrath of anyone in charge. In time, Leah would return and try to set things right. But right now, she needed to find her husband. She turned the headlights on, leaned back in the seat, and drove.

CHAPTER TWENTY-SIX

LEAH

Rose Valley Lane
    Smyrna, Georgia
    Sunday, 1:00 a.m.

The familiar sight of Leah's neighborhood unleashed a torrent of butterflies against her ribs. Thanks to Grant's trip to Charlotte and the terrible events of the weekend before, it had been ten days since she'd last set eyes on her husband.

Ten horrifying days.

She'd been through so much on her own, but it was all nearing an end. Leah eased the truck down the street and turned into her driveway. A pang of disappointment hit her when she didn't see Grant's car, but intellectually she knew better. Just like a million other cars all over the city, Grant's late-model Toyota didn't run.

It would probably sit at the Atlanta airport forever,

eventually succumbing to rain and rust and exposure. Leah put the truck in park and turned off the engine before bounding up the driveway and the two steps to her front door. She put her face up to the glass, but pulled back in shock.

Are those my new sheets?

She shook her head, squinting into the glass. Why had he used her sheets as window coverings? It didn't make sense. Leah tried the door handle. *Locked.* She knocked.

The noise echoed through the silent house.

She bounced on the balls of her feet, up and down, side to side, waiting.

Nothing. She frowned and pulled her backpack off before rummaging through it for her keys. At least she'd remembered to take them. The key fit into the lock and Leah opened the door.

Stale air greeted her. "Grant? Are you home?"

Leah eased inside and shut the door behind her. Complete darkness enveloped her. Her breath caught in her lungs. Even when the power failed, their first floor wasn't dark. The ambient light from the night always shined through the wall of windows in the back of the house.

Not tonight.

She called out again. "Grant? Honey, are you here?"

Leah fished in her bag for the hospital flashlight she'd managed to keep during the escape. She clicked it on. Plywood covered every window.

Leah spun around, panic rising in her throat. What

was going on? Every single window on the first floor had been barricaded. Leah didn't know what to think.

Had Grant done all this after the blast?

Leah walked into the kitchen in a trance. No sign of her husband. She searched the rest of the first floor, ducking into the bathroom and the office. *Not there.*

She took the stairs two at a time, racing against her own pounding heart. Their bed sat empty and cold. Her husband wasn't home.

Leah sagged onto the corner of the mattress, fighting back a wave of tears and despair. If he wasn't there, and he wasn't in Hampton, where the hell was he?

It was the middle of the night.

Exhaustion needled her, sparking a throb in the wound on her scalp. She needed to sleep, but she'd built up this moment so much in her mind: finally finding Grant, wrapping her arms around his strong middle, sinking into his chest.

Leah forced herself to stand and trudged back down the stairs. She tugged open the fridge and stared at the clean, bare shelves. She turned around and opened the cabinets.

Everything had been cleaned. No food sat rotting on the shelves. She opened the trash. A new bag.

A pair of dishes sat on the floor. Leah squatted down and squinted at the bowl half full of water. They didn't own a dog.

Leah shook her head. Nothing made sense. Where could he be?

The garage was the only place left. Leah walked to it,

prepared to find it empty. Instead, an old sedan sat on sagging tires in the middle of the space. She approached with caution and peered inside, but the car was empty.

If her husband had a working car, why wasn't he using it? She leaned over and shone a light on the front tire. A gash marred the side. Leah walked around the vehicle, inspecting each wheel.

The tires had been slashed. She stood up with a start. Who would do such a thing? A neighbor?

Leah didn't know what to do. She couldn't sleep. She couldn't think. She walked back into the house and picked up the air rifle. If someone would slash her husband's tires, what would they do when they found out he wasn't home?

She walked back out the front door and closed it softly behind her. A pair of rocking chairs nestled on Leah's front porch right where she left them and she sat in the one closest to the wall. From her vantage point, she could make out most of the street.

If she couldn't sleep she might as well stand guard. It didn't take long for exhaustion to overtake her nerves.

* * *

A metal clang roused Leah from quasi-unconsciousness. She blinked at the dark. *Where am I?* The air rifle slipped and banged against her shin and she jolted fully awake.

Her neighborhood. Her empty house. Her missing husband.

She heard the noise again, a metal-on-metal screech

coming from her driveway and the truck. Was someone trying to steal it? What if someone hot-wired it and drove off? She needed that truck to search for Grant. No one could take it from her.

Leah lifted the gun back up into her hands, all of a sudden alert and ready. "Is someone there?"

The noise cut off.

Leah squinted into the darkness, but even with the moon and stars, she couldn't make out any movement. Blood whooshed in her veins and her heart picked up speed. Leah didn't know if she could handle another altercation.

First Howie and then the men in the hospital. What would the next assailant do?

She eased off the rocking chair. "Hello? Are you out there?" With both hands firmly on the gun, she brought it up to her shoulder. If someone appeared, she wanted to be ready.

With quiet feet, she crept toward the edge of the porch and the driveway beyond. Thanks to the recessed front of the house and the looming hulk of the truck, Leah couldn't see the other side of the drive. Ten guys could be crouched over there and she'd have no idea.

Leah nosed around the engine. From her vantage point, she couldn't see anyone inside the cab. The doors were shut. She braced herself and swung into the open drive.

A shape hunched toward the back of the truck, bent over the wheel well.

Leah took aim. "Step away from the truck."

The shape jerked away. From the height and the bulk in his shoulders, Leah guessed it had to be a man, and a sizable one at that. She kept her voice firm and even. "Who are you?"

He didn't say anything.

"What are you doing?"

No response.

She bent her head toward the sights. "Talk or I fill your shoulder full of lead."

"I don't think there's any need for violence."

Leah couldn't place his voice and without more light, he was too far away to see. "Identify yourself."

"What if I refuse?"

She took a step forward. "You need to leave."

He took a step back. "I'm just having a look at the truck, that's all. Real classic."

"I wouldn't know."

"Does it run?"

"What do you think?"

He didn't respond.

Leah advanced another step. "If you don't leave, I'll shoot."

"Do you really know how to use that thing?"

She almost laughed. "You're not the first man I've had to shoot this week, so, yeah. I know how to use it."

The man's form shifted as he turned toward the truck.

"Stop moving."

He eased back upright. "I won't be much longer."

"That's right. Because you're leaving now."

"Not quite."

Leah couldn't figure him out. What was he doing standing beside the truck like that? She advanced another step. Another shape materialized out of the dark and Leah gasped. "You're stealing my gas!"

"I'd like to think I'm borrowing it."

"Get away."

The man picked up the plastic gas can from the ground and held it in front of his chest. "I need it."

"So do I."

"If you shoot me, we're both liable to explode." He yanked the tube from the gas tank out of the truck and wrapped both arms around the gas can, using it like a shield.

Leah didn't know what to do. She remembered all the signs at every gas station warning about the risk of explosions. She'd heard about gas cans spontaneously catching fire in weird places like hot garages and the trunks of cars in places like Phoenix or Las Vegas.

But outside Atlanta in the dark? It couldn't have been over sixty degrees. From the cold across her skin, Leah guessed more like fifty. Would the gas explode? If she aimed for his face, would she hit the tank on accident?

"Let me go and neither one of us gets hurt."

"No. Put down the can."

"I can't." The man took a step backward.

Leah took aim. With a good shot, she might incapacitate him enough to steal the can back. It was the best option. If he attacked her, she'd have to fight it out.

He wasn't stealing her gas.

The man backed up another step.

"Last chance. Put the gas down and walk away or I'm going to shoot."

The man didn't say anything.

Leah counted to ten. Then she aimed for his head. As her fingers tightened around the trigger, the sound of an engine stilled her hand. A single headlight lit up the road and the man standing in the middle of it.

CHAPTER TWENTY-SEVEN
GRANT

Rose Valley Lane
   Smyrna, Georgia
   Sunday, 1:00 a.m.

Grant had been driving for hours, trying to navigate the clogged streets of Atlanta without constantly using his headlight. The more he used it, the more he risked drawing attention to himself. One of these days, he'd draw the wrong kind of attention.

But with the middle of the night upon him, he'd given up and flicked it on. As he turned onto his street, the headlight lit up a man standing in the middle of the road. He was clutching a gas can to his chest.

Grant slowed. *Is he standing outside my house?* Grant looked up. An old beater of a truck sat in his driveway. Grant didn't have a clue what was going on. He reached for his Shield with one hand as he eased the bike to a stop.

The dog leapt from the milk crate and her ears flattened against the back of her head. Grant killed the engine and her growl filled the silence.

Grant walked up to the man. "Donny, is that you?"

The other man turned to Grant. "Hey."

"What's going on."

Donny hesitated. "I-I...didn't know you were home."

"I wasn't. Is that your truck?"

A voice carried out from around the other side of the truck as a shape emerged from the dark. "No. It's mine."

Grant almost fell to the ground. A woman stood in the light of the single headlight, head shaved and swollen with a nasty gash that looked infected. Dark circles ringed her eyes. A set of scratches marred her cheek.

But to Grant, she was the most beautiful thing he'd ever seen. "Leah?"

"Hey, honey." She smiled over the sight of a rifle. "Tell Donny to give me back my gas."

Grant turned to the man. He looked first at the gas can, and then the hose trailing out of the top, and finally, Donny's face. "Were you stealing her gas?"

"I...I need it."

"So does everyone. What made you think it was okay to take it?"

Donny clutched the red plastic tighter. "I'm out of food. I've got to get to a store."

"We all do. But stealing from a neighbor is not the way to make it happen. Give me the can."

"No!" Donny gripped it so hard the plastic dented.

Grant glanced at his wife. She was straight out of an action movie and just as bad-ass as any female heroine. He smiled before turning back to the thief and lifted the Shield into view. "I've got eight rounds of 9mm that say you will."

"You wouldn't risk it."

Grant took aim. "From here, I'm a dead shot. You'll take your last breath before you hit the ground."

Donny's head swiveled back and forth between Grant and Leah. At last, he released his grip on the can. "Fine. Take it."

Grant kept the gun trained on Donny as he reached with his free hand to take the can. As soon as he cleared it, he jerked his head toward the road. "Go home. And don't ever try to steal from us again."

Donny took off at a lumbering jog down Rose Valley Lane and out of sight. Once Grant was sure he was gone, he turned to his wife. "Let's go inside, huh?"

Leah didn't respond. The gun sagged in her grip.

"Honey? Are you okay?"

Her hand reached for her head as the gun slipped. It clattered onto the pavement and Grant darted forward.

He slipped an arm beneath Leah and caught her before she hit the ground. "Oh, babe. What's happened to you?" Grant kissed her bald head and scooped her limp body up into his arms. He opened the front door and carried his wife to the couch before laying her down. He checked for a pulse: weak, but steady.

Grant exhaled and the dog sat down beside him. He

turned to the dirty little thing. "Watch her for me. I'll be right back."

He ran out of the house and scooped up the gas can and Leah's rifle. He frowned at its weight. It wasn't the hunting rifle he'd assumed at first glance. She was risking her life with nothing more than an air rifle? They barely shot more than birdshot.

It would never have stopped a man Donny's size. Grant shook his head in amazement. He'd always known his wife possessed a quiet strength, but tending to the sick and dying was a far cry from pointing a toy of a gun at a man twice her size.

Grant rushed the things inside before hustling back out to the motorcycle. He wheeled it up the driveway and over the steps and into the entryway. There was no time to put it in the garage. Leah needed him.

After shutting and locking the front door, Grant rushed to the hall closet. He dug out the trauma kit Leah always stored in the house and found the flashlight clipped to the front. He ripped it off and clicked it on before heading back to the couch. The little dog moved back to give him room.

"How is she?"

Grant glanced at the dirty fluff ball. She spun around in a circle and lay down.

"Is that good or bad?"

He didn't have a clue. Grant stared at his wife's limp body. She was the nurse in this relationship. Grant could take care of cuts or scrapes or a headache, but passing out was outside of his wheelhouse. He reached forward and put a hand on her forehead.

Burning hot.

Grant leaned in to inspect his wife's head. The wound was swollen and angry with yellowed crust all around the base. Did that mean infection? *Probably*. Grant peered at the gash. Something clear caught the light.

Are those stitches? He swallowed and sat back on his heels. Had his wife shaved her own head and stitched herself up?

Grant didn't know what to do for infected sutures. Should he dig around in there and cut them out and irrigate the wound? Should he leave it and hope for the best?

He remembered her talking about people dying from secondary infections. A kid would scrape her leg while swimming in a river and rinse it off. A week later, she'd be barely breathing in intensive care, a staph infection wreaking havoc throughout her body.

Grant turned to the trauma kit. Taking up an entire military surplus backpack, Leah had stuffed it with everything she could use in an emergency and then some. There had to be something in there to bring her back.

With a deep breath, Grant unzipped it and stared. Leah had grouped all the supplies by type, stuffed them in gallon zippered bags, and labeled them. He rummaged through bandages and burn treatments and suture kits until he found the medicines.

Apart from ibuprofen, what would Leah use for a

head wound? *Antibiotics*. But those weren't shelf-stable. Grant frowned as he popped the medicine bag open and dumped the contents on the floor. He pushed the Benadryl and the Tylenol PM and tens of other medicines aside, searching without direction.

A bottle with brightly colored fish caught his eye. *Fish Mox* (*Amoxicillin*) *500 mg*. Grant swallowed and turned the bottle around and read the warning specifically against giving the medicine to humans.

He looked at his unconscious wife. They didn't own any fish. Leah didn't even like tuna. Why would she keep it in the trauma bag if she didn't mean for them to use it?

Grant pinched his lower lip between his fingers. He knew all about the problems with overprescribing antibiotics and bacterial resistance and what giving the wrong medication could do. Leah talked about it often.

But she never discussed what to do in a situation like this. Grant opened the bottle and popped the silver safety seal. He poured out a single pill and held it in his hand. "What should I do?"

The dog perked up and Grant turned toward her. "Do I give it to her or not?"

She stood up and padded over to Grant, sniffing the pill in his hand, before turning to look at Leah.

"Is that a yes?"

The dog barked once.

Grant shook his head. "I can't believe I'm taking advice from a dog, but here goes nothing." He stood up and grabbed one of his last bottles of water from the kitchen. "What doesn't kill you makes you stronger, right?"

He lifted his wife's head in his hand and forced her lips apart. As he gritted his teeth, he shoved the pill down her throat and followed it with a sip of water. Leah coughed and sputtered, but swallowed.

Grant eased her back down and resumed his position on the floor beside her head. He glanced at the dog. "It'll be all right. We just have to have faith."

CHAPTER TWENTY-EIGHT

LEAH

2078 Rose Valley Lane
Smyrna, Georgia
Sunday, 10:00 a.m.

Leah rubbed her eyes. What a dream. First, she'd stolen a truck and busted through a fence to escape a crazy town, then she'd faced off against a gas thief, and finally fallen into her husband's waiting arms. She'd had a few doozies now and again, but this dream topped them all.

A whine echoed through her brain and she almost laughed out loud. She'd forgotten about the mystery dog, too.

"Something funny?"

The sound of her husband's voice made her blink. She sat up and looked around. Whatever she was expecting to see, the dingy face of a little dog wasn't it. Leah tried not to panic. "What's going on?"

"You passed out last night on the street." Grant strode into the living room, holding a bottle of Gatorade and a bottle of pills. "I caught you before you hit the ground."

Leah blinked again. "You're real."

Grant raised an eyebrow. "Were you expecting something else?"

She ran her fingers over her lips. "I thought I was dreaming. You, the dog, coming home. All of it."

"Not a dream. I'm real." He smiled at the dog. "And so is she."

"Does she have a name?"

"Not yet."

Leah reached out her hand and the dog rose up to sniff it.

"I didn't think you wanted a dog."

"Didn't have much of a choice. She sort of came along for the ride." Grant eased down onto the edge of the couch. "I was thankful for the company."

"I'm thankful you're home."

"Same."

Grant leaned over and planted a small kiss on Leah's lips, and the part of her that had held it all together over the past week fell apart.

Tears leaked from her eyes and she snuffed back a sob. "I didn't know if I'd ever see you again. Where have you been?"

Grant shared the story of his journey from first hearing about the threat in the Hack-A-Thon in Charlotte, to hot wiring the Cutlass in the airport parking lot and driving a rental car employee home, to camping out with a bunch of long-haul truckers on the Georgia state line.

"That's incredible." She reached out and squeezed his hand. "You're lucky to be here."

"I know it." He handed her the Gatorade and Leah eased up to a sitting position. Her head ached but it didn't throb. She took a sip. "What's in the bottle?"

Grant turned it around until a pair of fish came into view. "I found it in the trauma bag and I forced you to swallow one last night."

Leah took the bottle and dumped another pill into her palm. "I'd forgotten I put these in there."

"It didn't kill you."

"It probably saved my life."

"So, I was right to give it to you?"

Leah popped the pill in her mouth and swallowed it down with some Gatorade. "Definitely. Fish antibiotics aren't as good as people ones since they aren't regulated, but my thinking is clearer, and my head doesn't feel like jackhammers are forcing their way through my skull."

Grant smiled. "Tell me about where you've been. I ran into a Dr. Phillips who said you had a car, but that's not what's in the driveway."

Leah lit up. "You found Andy? He's alive?"

"Helping out at a midtown pop-up nursing station." Grant leaned in. "He told me to tell you he's quit smoking for good."

Leah leaned back on the couch in relief. "I should be there, too."

"You have a nasty head wound. You're not going anywhere."

After another few sips of Gatorade, Leah explained everything that happened after the EMP, from the double shift at the hospital to the old man obsessed with *Seinfeld* to her escape from Hampton.

"I'm sorry about your sister."

"It's okay. I've come to terms with it. Maybe once things calm down, we'll be able to visit."

Her husband focused on his hands. "I'm not sure anything is going to calm down."

"Have you seen any signs of the government? Or aid?"

"None. Have you?"

"No." Leah leaned forward on the couch. "Doesn't that seem weird to you? Why isn't there a repeating broadcast on the radio or a line of Humvees rolling through town?"

Her husband scratched his head. "I don't think there's a whole lot of functioning government left."

Leah shuddered. "So, we're on our own?"

"Sure seems that way."

Leah couldn't think about any of that now. What mattered was that she was home with her husband. Together at last. They were alive. They had shelter.

They could survive.

Grant gave her another kiss on the temple before standing up. "You should go back to sleep. The more you rest, the faster you'll heal."

She smiled. "Yes, Nurse Walton."

He chuckled. "I learned from the best."

Leah lay back down and watched her husband walk away. She didn't know what they would do from here on out. If the power never came back on and the government didn't swoop in and assist, millions of people would begin to starve.

Riots. Looting. Mass chaos. It would all play out like a zombie movie without the reanimated dead. Soon there would be more bodies than living, breathing Americans.

But Leah couldn't think about any of that now. She had her husband. She had her home. That would have to be enough. They would find a way to not only live through the coming days, but to thrive. There would be an America after this.

Somehow. Someway. Grant whistled for the dog and Leah closed her eyes.

CHAPTER TWENTY-NINE

GRANT

2078 Rose Valley Lane
  Smyrna, Georgia
  Sunday, 12:00 p.m.

Even bald and wounded his wife stole his breath. She was the warrior in their pairing, not him. Grant reached down and scratched the dog as she bounded to a stop by his side. "Let's finally give you a bath, huh?"

He called the little thing up the stairs and into the master bathroom. After filling the tub with soap and water he motioned for her to hop in. The dog stared at the bath in trepidation.

"Oh, come on. You'll be happy to be clean."

She didn't move.

Grant blew out a breath. "If you get in the bath, I'll give you some jerky I pilfered from the sporting goods store."

The dog stepped forward and Grant shook his head. "You're unbelievable." He helped her clear the edge of the tub and set to work, rubbing lather along her back and rinsing the soap again and again. With every cup full of water, the dog's fur lightened.

After a few minutes, Grant leaned back. "Well, I'll be." Where a dingy gray dog once stood, a bright white dog now beamed. With her mouth open and blue eyes shining, she might as well have been smiling.

Grant ruffed her fur and the dog hopped out of the dirty water. He tossed a towel on her back and she shook from tip to tail. After he dried her off, the little dog's fur stuck out in all directions like a perfect snowball from fresh powder.

"She's beautiful."

Grant glanced up to find his wife leaning against the door frame, a blanket wrapped around her shoulders. "Do you think she's a Samoyed?"

Leah shook her head. "Too small. One just like her won best in show of the toy group. She's an American Eskimo Dog."

Grant scratched at his head. Fancy name for a stalwart little thing.

"Have a name yet?"

He stared at the fluff ball, so happy to be free of dirt. He thought about all the times she stood by his side. So patiently waiting for it to be her turn. He glanced up at his wife. "Faith. I think her name is Faith."

Leah lowered into a crouch and held out her hand.

"It's nice to meet you, Faith." The dog scampered over and gave her hand a lick.

Watching the pair of them laugh and snuggle broke the last bit of pain free from his heart. His wife was alive. They were together again. He pinched the bridge of his nose to keep from crying. "What are we going to do?"

Leah looked up with a solemn smile. "Take it one day at a time. It's all any of us can do now."

Faith's ears pricked as a banging sounded downstairs. "What's that?"

Grant stood up and listened. "It sounds like someone's knocking on the front door."

"Should I stay here?"

Grant shook his head. "No. Let's all go. Whatever happens, we'll face it together."

Discover what happens now that Grant and Leah are reunited in *Survive the Panic*:

With no help in sight, could you make the hard choices?

After risking everything, Grant and Leah Walton are finally reunited. But it's no happy ending. Without food, water, or any serious defenses, they're starting from scratch while their neighborhood falls apart. Will they have the strength to survive the ensuing panic? Or will the chaos of post-apocalyptic America be their undoing?

The attack is only the beginning.

* * *

Want to know how it all started? Subscribe to Harley's newsletter and receive *First Strike*, the prequel to the *Nuclear Survival* saga, absolutely free.

www.harleytate.com/subscribe

If you found out the world was about to end, what would you do?

Four ordinary people—a computer specialist, a hacker, a reporter, and a private investigator—are about to find out. Each one has a role to play in the hours leading up to the worst attack in United States history.

Will they rise to the occasion or will the threat of armageddon stop them in their tracks?

ACKNOWLEDGMENTS

Whoa.

Lots of things have happened this spring. I passed the one year mark of writing survival fiction, published my eighth novel, launched audiobooks for the first time, and hit massive author burn-out. Turns out raising three littles and keeping a up an eight-book-a-year pace is a bit more challenging than I expected!

So my sincere apologies on the delay between *Brace for Impact* and *Escape the Panic*. I've realized if I want to keep up writing for the long-term, I have to slow it down. This book was one of the hardest I've written since it takes place where I call home. I took lots of "research" trips all over not just Atlanta, but North Georgia parsing out how I wanted to tell this story.

With that in mind, please note that names and details of real places have been changed! Although I try to be as realistic as possible, I do take liberties with regard to names, places, and events for the sake of the story (and to not ruffle real life feathers!). I hope you don't object and can still go along for the ride.

If you enjoyed this book and have a moment, please consider leaving a review on Amazon. Every one helps new readers discover my work and helps me keep writing the stories you want to read.

Book three in the series will be out this summer.

Until then,

Harley

ABOUT HARLEY TATE

When the world as we know it falls apart, how far will you go to survive?

Harley Tate writes edge-of-your-seat post-apocalyptic fiction exploring what happens when ordinary people are faced with impossible choices.

The apocalypse is only the beginning.

Contact Harley directly at:
www.harleytate.com
harley@harleytate.com

Made in the USA
Columbia, SC
14 June 2024

37022702R00136